BARREL OF LIES

BARREL OF LIES

Charlie Gardner

AuthorHouse™ UK Ltd.
1663 Liberty Drive
Bloomington, IN 47403 USA
www.authorhouse.co.uk
Phone: 0800.197.4150

© 2013 by Charlie Gardner. All rights reserved.

No part of this book may be reproduced, stored in a retrieval system, or transmitted by any means without the written permission of the author.

Published by AuthorHouse   11/18/2013

ISBN: 978-1-4918-8350-1 (sc)
ISBN: 978-1-4918-8351-8 (e)

Any people depicted in stock imagery provided by Thinkstock are models, and such images are being used for illustrative purposes only.
Certain stock imagery © Thinkstock.

This book is printed on acid-free paper.

Because of the dynamic nature of the Internet, any web addresses or links contained in this book may have changed since publication and may no longer be valid. The views expressed in this work are solely those of the author and do not necessarily reflect the views of the publisher, and the publisher hereby disclaims any responsibility for them.

All characters in this publication are fictitious and any resemblance to persons living or dead is purely coincidental.

Dedicated to the lovely young ladies at Ark. Agne, Anne, Irene, Angela and Shelley, with a special mention for Leanne who puts the care in to carer. Angels to the devil incarnate. Thank you just does not cover it.

CHAPTER 1

"Hard decisions to be made Chas old boy," I said to myself. I was at the crossroads of a business decision that would possibly shape the rest of my life. I was fifty-two and either going to have more money than I ever felt possible, or I would be on a fraud charge, even, possibly jail. Not bad for an ex copper.

I rose from my office chair and descended the stairs to the ground floor level. The bar was buzzing with the usual crowd of friends' acquaintances and casual passers by.

"Watch out Sue, the boss is here. No more giving away free drinks." The speaker turned towards me, "didn't think you worked on Wednesday nights Chas. What's up no woman to keep you occupied tonight? Oh no, its your keep fit night ain't it?"

Steve, the first customer I served when I opened the pub nearly five years ago. Local man who at thirty-five, was nearly seventeen years younger than me. Called in for a drink every evening, except Sundays. Always on his own apart from Saturdays when his wife, Tina, accompanied him. Considered himself a bit of a Jack the lad, but he never strayed far from the straight and narrow, Tina saw to that. The beer he consumed showed on his waistline. Still his girth was my profit. About five feet nine and weighing fifteen stone he was the opposite of his wife who was five feet seven inches, and weighing a trim and shapely seven and a half stone. Tina liked to dress up but he had forbidden her to wear high heels on Saturday nights in the pub, following an evening when she towered over him and he was the butt of the being under the thumb jokes. He was fast losing his hair whereas Tina had long red tresses that set off her green eyes.

"Not tonight Steve got too much to think about. I'm not staying; I'm on my way to the gym. Wouldn't hurt you to join and spend a few hours in there each week."

"Not for me, the only spare time I have would eat into my drinking time. I may not live as long as you fitness freaks, but I will die happy."

I laughed and went out to my car where my kit was already waiting on the passenger seat. My normal fitness regime was a five-mile jog in the morning, every morning except Sundays and the gym twice a week. A few years ago I had doubts whether I would ever walk again without the aid of sticks or even a limp. I started the car, drove three streets away, and parked up. It was already beginning to get dark and I climbed out of the car leaving my kit on the seat. I would not need it; I was a mile from the fitness centre. Tonight was not my gym night either, although anybody who knew me thought it was.

I walked two streets on and entered a short drive to a smart semi detached dormer bungalow. I rang the bell. An attractive lady answered the door and led me through to a sitting room. She was dressed in a tight woollen sweater and figure hugging jeans that accentuated her slim but curvy body.

"Grab a pew, I'll get you a glass of red." I took a seat and waited for a glass of red wine to arrive. Considering the actions that were taking place over the next few days, then I guessed there would be a few regrets, and she was one of them.

"You've got a worried look on your face Chas, is there something wrong?"

"Nothing that an hour or so with you won't cure." I smiled at her and took a long drink from the glass of wine.

She took my hand. "Well if I can only have you for an hour, we'd better not waste time. Come on lets go upstairs." She picked up her glass and the bottle of wine.

Half dragged, I followed Tina upstairs to the bedroom, being careful not to spill my drink.

CHAPTER 2

Twelve years earlier

"Well guv, you happy enough for us to proceed?"

"Okay Chas, but be careful, Oldfield can be a dangerous bastard. I don't want any casualties, not even so much as Wendy moaning about a split fingernail. Go on, join the troops and get it underway."

This operation had taken me four months to put together. Sammy Oldfield was an ex army guy, dishonourably discharged for striking an officer, well not one officer but three, two captains, and a major who he had come across in a restaurant. One of the captains had looked down his nose at Oldfield's companion, she was a bit of a slut, and she and Oldfield had been drinking earlier, and he was on a promise. He could possibly have avoided the dishonourable discharge, if he had left it at only hitting the captain that made the disparaging remark. Unfortunately, after spreading the captain's nose all over his face, he laid in to the major and the other captain, who together had tried to pull him away, seriously injuring both of them. The army should have been proud of how well they had trained this man, but they were not. Years earlier, he had been decorated as a hero during the Falklands war conflict. A spell in the glasshouse at Colchester, followed by his discharge, was the end of Sergeant Oldfield's military career.

Not finding employment on his release, he resorted to robbery with violence. Somehow he managed to avoid arrest, always moving on after a few days, sometimes staying with old army mates, other times sleeping rough.

His luck changed when an ex soldier who had joined the force, spotted him in a park taking slugs of cider from a bottle. Regrettably, he spotted the constable and was away on his toes before the officer could affect an arrest. Drunk or otherwise, he was fit and fleet of foot.

With everybody in stab vests and helmets, the group made their way to Oldfield's hiding place, a run down Victorian semi detached bed and breakfast. As luck would have it, another resident was leaving as the police arrived. Surprised by the number of officers pushing past him, he hurried away down the street, anxious not to be caught up in what was going down. Instructing the others, except for three officers, one carrying a door opener, to stay downstairs, Chas knocked on the door of Oldfield's first floor room. "Police Mr Oldfield. Open the door." He waited a moment, repeated the words again then motioned for the officer with the heavy weighted door opener to proceed.

It took two strikes for the door to give way. Two officers rushed in. Nothing, although intelligence gained from surveillance, said he was in the building. The other officers joined the search. They split themselves between the ground floor and the two upstairs floors. A couple of minutes later the downstairs was declared clear. He had to be upstairs, but where? Surveillance had said he returned at elevenish last night and had not been seen to leave. Two helmeted heads appeared at the top of the stairs. "No sign of him here sarge, should we get a dog in. The only place we haven't looked is the loft."

"Carry on looking, I'm coming up." I climbed the stairs and looked in the first room. The two officers were checking the wardrobes for false back panels. I left and took another room. Bare floorboards, a single bed with mattress, but no covers. The ceilings were tall, three and a half metres or more, with wardrobes all along one wall, nearly reaching the ceiling. I searched them, then turning to leave, I almost bumped in to DC Wendy Johnson who had entered the room.

"You should stay downstairs, until the area is declared safe." I gave her a stern look.

As I walked past her, there was movement as a body leapt from the top of the robes and grabbed Wendy. I turned to see Oldfield holding Wendy with his left arm and waving a gun in his right hand. Oldfield was not particularly tall at five feet ten inches, but quite powerfully built at twelve stone. His head was shaved, and a barbed wire tattoo circled his neck. He was in his usual garb of camouflage T-shirt and fatigues.

"Well, well, Chas Barker. Should have guessed this would be your caper. Now get out of my way, me and the delightful young lady are going to leave, and you lot are going to step aside. You'd better let your mates know before I have to shoot someone."

I called out to the others then moved inside the room away from the door. "Give yourself up, you don't stand a chance."

"I've already spent four years inside. I ain't doing that again. I'd rather die."

He pushed Wendy to the landing at the top of the stairs. There were two flights of stairs, the first of seven steps then a ninety-degree turn and a further ten or so, to the next floor. He grasped her around the neck and she stepped down to the next tread. Oldfield now stood head and neck above her. I could not believe my eyes as she arched her backside in to him, and reached up, grabbing the arm around her throat and pulled him over her. This sent the two of them tumbling and twisting as they crashed down to the next landing. A shot was fired as they plummeted over each other. They hit the wall, him on top of her, his gun still in his hand. I rushed from the room and jumped landing on top of them both, fearing that he was going to shoot again. As I did, Oldfield fired. My momentum carried me in to him, with my left boot catching his gun hand and knocking the weapon free. Before I had gathered my senses, other officers were restraining and cuffing Oldfield and pulling him and me free of Wendy, who was making loud groaning noises.

"Christ woman what the bloody hell made you do that? I couldn't believe what I was seeing. Are you all right?"

"I was until you jumped on top of us. I think I've cracked a rib and I can feel a lump on my head the size of a football."

"Thank God for that. I feared the worst when the gun went off as you both tumbled down the stairs. Christ you scared me. Didn't you realise he could have killed you. As it is my heart is beating so fast, I could suffer a heart attack."

I was sat on the step above Wendy. "Here let me give you a hand to get up." I tried to rise but my left leg collapsed under me sending me crashing on top of Wendy again. She put out a hand, both to protect herself, and cushion my fall.

She pulled her hand back as I lay to her side. She looked at her hand, then me. "Fucking hell sarge you're bleeding. You've been hit." She pulled out her mobile and called for an ambulance.

CHAPTER 3

I spent the next twelve weeks in hospital. The bullet had been fired up towards me and had entered under the hem of the stab vest. Hitting the top of my thigh and hip, it then travelled on catching my liver slightly and then my spleen, plus anything else it could find in between. My spleen was now incinerated free of charge by the hospital, maybe I was going to be cremated piece by piece. However, I was told my liver was healing. My hip had been repaired with the skill of a surgeon come mechanical engineer. The worst part was the traction and physiotherapy. The best part was the R and R and being waited on hand and foot. I had not been looked after like this since my wife had left me three years ago. Now I was at home hobbling around with the aid of a stick.

To begin with there were a great number of colleagues and friends who called to aid my recovery, but as it dragged on the figure dropped to a couple of close friends and relatives, with the odd visit from Wendy and my governor, DI Chivers.

The big surprise was a visit from my sister, Fay, who lived in Spain. Fay was forty-eight, eight years older than me. I had not seen her for six years, although we had both promised to visit on a regular basis, Fay only stayed for three days, but we did an awful lot of catching up. She left telling me that as soon as I was fit I should go over and stay with her for some R and R. She also visited my mother. They had got on well when Fay lived at home and I know they spoke every three days or so on the telephone

After another three months, my internals were given the all clear, but my walking was far from right and anything more than a fast stroll was ungainly. I both looked and felt as if I would go arse overhead. Although I could not care or less, both Wendy and I received commendations for bravery. I was pleased for Wendy though.

Now fourteen months later, I was discussing my future with my Chief Superintendent, my old DI, and some tall thin faced fellow from human resources. I could tell from the drift of the meeting that my CS wanted me out of his office; the chap from HR was looking at saving the force money, and my boss DI John Chivers was there to hold my hand.

There were choices. The offer of an office job, which was as appealing as a poke in the eye with a rusty nail. Invalided out of the force with a cash lump sum and a full pension. Undergo further tests and with medical and legal advice consider where my future lie. No immediate answer was required, but I was left under no illusion that earlier rather than later was the desired outcome.

The CS and the HR chap left, but the DI stayed behind.

"Chas, all they want is to remove your cost off their part of the balance sheet. I'd love you back 'cos I want a bloody good DS to keep my troops in order, and heading in the right direction on investigations. Your decision must be what you want. Take your time, they can't or won't push you."

"I know that guv, I had a fed rep come round and give me the low down on my rights. Now I let them see all the medical reports. My insides ain't too bad but I couldn't run to save my life. That they say makes me a risk. The last thing I want is a desk job, it just ain't me. At the moment I'm on full pay but in a few months that could drop to half, that's when I'll decide. I'm saving most of my pay. Other than pay my usual bills, I spend only a very little. I go for a walk twice a day and to the hospital for physio twice a week. No pub and very few meals out."

"Bloody hell, never known you to be so clean living, and you're saving money. And, you've lost that beer belly. Bullets! They're not all grief are they. Don't let my wife know or she'll want me to take one and be confined to hospital."

"The worst thing is feeling so well but incapable of doing much. I'll give it these next few months to see how much progress I make then decide what the rest of my life has for me."

"Well as I said, you don't have to make a decision now, let the buggers wait. Sorry Chas but I have to be on my way, but I will pop in again soon. Look after yourself and don't put off calling in to the station, there's lot of people would be glad to see you."

I showed John out and then went and collected the dirty cups and saucers to wash up.

There followed another six months of treatment, and I was now being asked again to consider my future. In all honesty, I was not sure. Being at home with no real responsibilities had not provided any incentive to give it a lot of thought.

The Police Federation had informed me that with their doctor's report and their help, I should be able to get a cash lump sum and a full pension, if that was what I wanted. I could also get a desk job, but further progression in my career would be limited. I was forty-one and at a crossroads in my life and I had no idea where I was going.

CHAPTER 4

Life took an unexpected turn, when, on one of my visits to the physiotherapist, I bumped in to a chap who I had met during an investigation many years earlier. Martin Bishop owned a few pubs and restaurants and he had called the police in when he suspected someone was dealing drugs on his premises. I was leaving the treatment area as he was entering.

"DS Barker isn't it?"

"Was, I'm just plain Mr Barker now. You're Martin Bishop aren't you? Should remember, there's a file a foot thick on you back at the nick."

"What?" He looked astonished. "Why would they have a file on me?"

"Only joking. If there is a file, they never showed it to me. How are you keeping, still in the pub trade?"

"For my sins." He looked enquiringly at me. "Mister Barker? You no longer a copper then? I'd have guessed you were there for the long term. Why'd you leave or is that not the right question?"

"Nothing wrong with the question. I got injured and am now unfit for duty. That's why I spend time here."

"Are you working?" I shook my head. "Well in that case if you're interested in getting a job, call round The Potters for a chat any time next week. Look I need to rush otherwise I'll be charged double for being late. Don't forget, any time next week. Nice to have seen you again." With that, he disappeared through the door and out of sight.

A job, I had not given much thought to working again. I had a tidy sum in the bank and my pension. I had paid off my mortgage and my income was more than adequate for my needs. Still, something to occupy my mind and get the brain functioning again. The idea became appealing.

The thought of working again put a spring in my step, and I decided that instead of taking a bus, I would walk the two or three miles back home. Reaching home, I was ready for a cup of tea, but today there was something missing. I did not reach for the painkillers that were often necessary after a visit for physiotherapy, and I had walked home. Life was getting better.

I took my cup of tea and sat at the table pondering over what sort of job Martin Bishop was likely to offer me. Barman? Look after security for his empire? Personal assistant? Of course, it may just be a potman in one of his watering holes. Whatever, I would find out next week.

The following week I called round at The Potters to see Martin. An old-fashioned type of pub with a public bar that I thought had disappeared from the licensed trade and a saloon bar, that at one end doubled as a restaurant. You could also get food in the public bar, but it was limited to meals in a basket, plus a few other quick meals, usually with chips. For a midweek lunchtime, it was reasonably busy with office types. Not all of them were in the saloon, as it appeared some enjoyed a raucous game of darts with their pint and a snack. Martin took me through to his office upstairs.

"I'm glad you decided to come, and I hope you're going to choose to help me." I was about to say something but he continued, "Don't say anything yet, hear me out then ask all the questions you like." He proceeded to let me know what he had in mind and I kept quiet whilst he explained the problems he was encountering.

"Christ Almighty Martin, you're not asking for much are you? I don't know anything about the pub trade and as for the protection racket; don't you think you ought to go to the police? I'm retired and I ain't fit enough to go up against a couple of heavies. I need to think about this. I may be able to sort the first puzzle but other than advice I don't know about the second."

"I'm not expecting you to take on these hooligans, just see if you can find a way of getting rid of them. I say protection because that's all I think it can be, but there haven't been any demands for money or anything else for that matter. Think about it for a few days and let me know. I'm not going to mention money now, but the amount I'm willing to pay won't disappoint you. Plus, I'm not averse to making the position permanent. I need somebody to keep an eye on the pubs and clubs. I've got six bars, a restaurant and a share in a nightclub. Still that's enough about business today, let's go downstairs and I'll have the chef rustle up a lunch. You may as well have something for giving me your time today."

Downstairs, at a quiet table at the rear of the saloon, but not in the restaurant we settled down to a diet coke each while we waited for his chef to prepare us some fish. You could tell the food was for the boss, for when it came it was platter of scallops, squid rings, garlic prawns and fish goujons with a side salad, chunky chips and crusty bread.

"So if I work for you, do I get to eat and drink for free?" I asked.

"If it persuades you to take the job, yes. I'll make an allowance for how much you'll eat when I figure out what to pay you. Most of the staff grab something to eat during their shift. I don't mind, especially if they're good workers, and the bad ones don't last long. In this business, you need good people and if I find someone, I try to hang on to them. Customers like it too if they recognise faces, it's more relaxing."

We finished our food, shook hands, and I promised to let him know within a couple of days. Leaving the pub, I decided to walk for a while before catching a bus home.

That evening, although I tried to put my meeting with Martin Bishop out of my mind, by watching a television programme on space travel, I could not shake off the idea of getting a job and going back to work. Being off all that time had its advantages. For the first time I had enjoyed every televised match from Italia 90. Even if England had been beaten by Germany on penalties in the semi finals. Germany then went on to beat Argentina in what was probably the most boring match in World Cup finals ever. England lost third place to the host nation 2-1. In the end, I fell asleep in the armchair and did not wake until one thirty in the morning.

CHAPTER 5

Rising the next morning, I felt as stiff as a board, and then remembered that I had fallen asleep in the armchair. The odd thing was, that my stiff neck and back removed the ache I usually felt from my hip in the morning. I took a couple of co-proximal tablets hoping they would do for my neck and back what they did for my hip.

Following some toast and a cup of tea, I went for my daily walk. The newsagents was only two streets away, but I took a half hour stroll to get there, then a brisk ten minute walk home to spend the next hour or so reading the paper with a cup of coffee. Today however I could not concentrate on the newspaper. Thoughts of returning to work kept invading my thoughts. Not being able to focus on anything else made my mind up for me. I would see Martin on Monday, and unless between now and then I thought of something to give me reason to say no, then I would be in paid employment again.

Monday came and I again went to The Potters to see Martin. "Well if the job offer is still there then I'm applying for it." I said.

"Fantastic. I was hoping you'd say yes. If you have time, I'll show you around the pubs, well three of them and the club. We won't have time to do all of them. Have you got the time?"

"My diaries free. I don't have many commitments in my life except for hospital visits, which reminds me, they will continue for a while yet, so half a day a week I will be at the clinic. Which pubs are we visiting today?"

"I thought we'd start with the most run down ones and the newest acquisition. It needs some work, mostly cosmetic. You'll see when we get there. Come on let's make a move. My cars round the back."

We drove out towards Guildford, in the late summer sun, until we came to a village, or at least it was before they added two largish housing estates, one of which was still in course of construction. Martin explained, "This place was a small village backwater, and the local was losing money and about to be shut down by the brewery. I heard on the quiet about the likelihood of the new housing and made them an offer, well below asking price and valuation, and they took it. It needs improvement, which will happen once the builders have left. At the moment we have a dozen or so regular customers, mostly builders from the site, every weekday lunchtime. I also discovered most don't drink during the day except for soft drinks, and soft drinks carry high margins. And of course they buy grub. I'll be sorry when they go, but hopefully by then, with the houses sold, I'll have new customers."

We pulled in at The Falcon. "Welcome to The Falcon at Lower Upwood, the only pub within five miles."

The Falcon must have been one of the oldest buildings in the village. Whitewashed walls and black timbers, excepting a brick built extension to the side, which rather spoilt the oldy worlde look. Parking at the side of the road, we entered through a small porch in to a large open area that was broken up by low brick walls, on which stood heavy timbers that appeared to be structural supports. There were three or groups of men sat around at tables tucking in to various dishes.

A barman called out. "Behave yourself lads the boss has called in to check you out. No fighting, mooning, swearing or spitting until he's gone." The men laughed and one shouted back, "Does that mean we have to stop ogling the staff?"

"Yes, you're not to make lewd comments or stare at Sarah's bust until he's gone."

"Not Sarah, John, it's you we fancy," came back a rejoinder.

John was about forty years old, slightly balding with sandy coloured hair. He was quite tall at about six feet with a stocky build. His short-sleeved shirt showed his well-developed biceps. He grinned as Martin and I stepped over to the bar. Martin introduced us, but did not let on that I was joining the business.

"Hi John, this lot behaving themselves?" John nodded; Martin introduced me, but did not let on that I was joining the business.

Martin leant over towards John and quietly asked if they had paid for their meals yet. John shook his head. Martin turned towards to the men at the tables. "Food is on the house today lads and get yourselves another drink to."

A cheer broke out, and shouts of thanks.

Martin ordered a couple of diet cokes and two plates of whatever Sarah had cooking in the kitchen. We made our way to a table in the corner.

"That's a nice gesture," I said.

"Yes and no," replied Martin. "They have spent a considerable amount here over the last year or so. When I took this place on we had a few niggles with electrics and plumbing and some of those lads fixed things for John. He has a good relationship with them as does Sarah his partner, who does the cooking and waiting. You'll meet her in a moment. Lovely woman. Attractive too. If you look around you'll notice the paint needs freshening up, and this carpet is so old its like tar and stuck to the floor. There's no pile on it. Kitchen will have to be completely renewed, but if I'm right there should be enough customers locally to justify the expenditure."

A moment later Sarah appeared with two plates of sausages and mash with a jug of onion gravy. Simple it may have been but it smelt delicious.

Sarah had red hair not ginger, but bottle red, almost an aubergine colour. I also saw the relevance of John's remark to stop ogling the barmaid. She had a large bust, not grossly enormous but big enough to give any man sinful thoughts. Looking just like a good barmaid should she was wearing a v necked sweater which displayed her cleavage and a loose wrap around skirt. Definitely a woman to turn heads.

"I can guess what you're thinking so forget it, John would kill you, he's ex Para. All punters like to flirt with her and she plays them along, not nastily but with humour. John trusts her one hundred per cent and often has a chuckle at some of the antics. Both were working for a chain when I met them and it took about five minutes for me to decide I wanted him working for me. He wasn't sure to begin with but in the end he said yes. I sent them both on a training course and gave them a pub just outside Windsor to manage. It was often frequented by squaddies from the local barracks, and used to be a bit of a problem. Within two months of John taking over the trouble stopped but we hadn't lost the custom, in fact it increased when others realised it was now a decent pub to have a pint in. All staff I take on spend three months with him and Sarah, to understand how to run a good pub."

The construction gang got up to go but each made a point of approaching our table and saying thanks to Martin. I could see it pleased him.

After leaving The Falcon we visited two other pubs, but these were considerably smarter and first impressions were that they were well run.

Club OMG was a different kettle of fish, situated just off Princess Way in Camberley. It was in rows of shops, that in some cases were boarded up. Last in the row the club was next to a few terraced properties, but most of these looked to be unoccupied. A number had been demolished and the land cleared. It looked as though commuters and shoppers had taken the space over as a car park. The front of the club was painted in a dark green, with gold lettering. Not garish by any means, but in such a run down area it stood out. Inside was like a lot of clubs, in daylight with all the lights on, a little on the seedy side. Of course at night with subdued lighting and coloured spots, it was transformed in to a magical kingdom where young people had fun and enjoyed themselves. There was a galleried floor around and above the dance floor. The downstairs space was basically that, other than a bar about fifty feet long against the far wall. The walls either side had fixed sofa style seating.

"Nice club Martin, but the areas a bit tatty. Still I don't suppose the kids worry about that."

"They love it, and they're not really kids. You have to be over twenty two to get in here and yes we do check their ID's. Being here without too much by way of neighbours to aggravate makes it an ideal site. When we close, I have security keep an eye on the immediate area to stamp out any hassle. This place generates a good income so we need to hang on to our licence. It's a pity we're a little early for you to meet Zac, my manager, but the hours are late in a place like this so he won't be in till early evening."

We spent another twenty minutes or so chatting and viewing the two offices, cloakroom, toilets, cellar and storerooms before Martin said we'd have to go as he had an appointment in North Camp, but that he'd drop me off in Wokingham on the way through.

We were driving back through Sandhurst when I said to Martin, "it was very nice seeing a couple of pubs and clubs, but what exactly will my job be? You don't seem to have any problem that I can see."

"There is no problem with the three pubs you have seen but of the other three one is not making the margins it should and I'd like you to look in to it."

"Well I'll do what I can but I'm not an accountant. Still if it gets to complicated, I'll let you know and we can get a chap I knew in the force who's a genius with figures. He's not a copper but works freelance, unless of course you have someone already."

"No Chas, as long as the cost isn't prohibitive you'll have a free hand. My other problem concerns the restaurant and club. A few months ago my people on door security at the club realised a group of hoodlums were looking to cause trouble. Errol, the chief security honcho, spotted that something was going on and with the help of the other stewards, rounded them up and showed them the door. A couple of weeks later the same thing happened again but not before there had been a bit of a fight. Errol recognised one of them from the previous encounter and took his photo and made sure the CCTV DVD was locked away in to the safe. A month after, that on a Thursday evening, a group of diners at the restaurant were noisy and disruptive and when Laurence, he's the manager asked them to leave, they kicked off, knocking over chairs and tables and threatening the other diners. One of the chefs is an old friend of John at The Falcon; they were in the paras together, and when he stepped in to help Laurence, they were soon shown the door."

"Are you telling me that it's the same gang?"

"There's a bit more yet. Just like the club, about two weeks later there was another fracas at the restaurant with a few more tables and chairs broken and a few more disgruntled customers. On both occasions, the police have looked at the CCTV but they don't think they're a local gang, so nothing has happened. Once again, a couple of the faces on the CCTV go back to the club disturbance. I just feel as if I'm being targeted."

"Have there been any demands for cash?" I enquired.

"Like I said before, nothing at all. That's what's so frustrating."

"Have you upset anybody because it's not common knowledge that the club and restaurant are both owned by you, even if only partly in the case of the club. Get me copies of the security DVD's so that I can have a butchers, and then I'll start to make a few enquiries."

"You still haven't asked me how much I'm going to pay you. I'm hoping you will be happy with thirty-five K per annum plus car and benefits. I'm not expecting you to work forty hours a week, just give me fair return on my money. Don't answer now call round at The Potters tomorrow and I'll have the DVD's and you can tell me what you think then. If it's okay with you I'll drop you here so I don't have to find my way back to this road. The walk will do you good!" He pulled up outside the Guide Dog training centre and I got out saying I would see him tomorrow.

CHAPTER 6

"I need you to step up the softening up process against Bishop. I don't care how you do it but I want him to know someone has him in their sights." The speaker was Billy Maggs.

Maggs was a small time crook turned property developer. Although only five feet five inches and looking as if a stiff breeze would blow him over, he began as an enforcer for Jimmy Briggs who ran protection rackets, drugs and prostitutes. Not over-powerful, he was always accompanied by a slow-witted man mountain called Budgie. When Jimmy Briggs was killed in a drug deal that went wrong, Billy took over with Budgie's help. No one was ever charged with the murder and the gun was never found. Maggs persuaded the crime lord who brought his drugs from Jimmy, to pay him a hundred thousand for the uncut heroin Jimmy had stashed away, and for the list of contacts. The rackets and girls brought in a steady income, but he wanted something more solid. Property.

"I'll let the boys know and we'll increase the hurt. I won't let you down Mr Maggs."

"Make sure you don't, and one further thing, none of this is to be traced back to me."

"It won't, the boys don't know who they're doing this for and never will, not from me."

Maggs put the phone down.

※

"Bloody hell, you start early don't you. It's only just gone eight. Hang on I'll come down." The voice belonged to Amy, the assistant manager of The Potters and wife of Barry Hopkins, the manager. She was leaning out of an upstairs window dressed in a cardigan and not much else from what I could see. "You need to go round the back I'm not opening the bar doors."

I started to say that I would come back later but the window had closed and Amy was gone. I made my way to the back only to find my path blocked by a wrought iron gate that was padlocked. A voice came from the back of the building. "Come on. Where the bloody hell are you?"

I called back. "The gates locked, I can't get through."

"Hold on a minute I'll have to find my slippers."

A few moments later Amy appeared round the corner of the pub muttering under her breath. What exactly I could not make out, but I think I was the target of her ire. She was still dressed in the jumper, and as I now discovered a pair of knickers. Unlocking the gate she let me through not bothering to relock it but snapping the padlock shut so that nobody could remove it.

Like all managed pubs, the back door led to stairs that took you to the first floor that was the living accommodation, and in the case of The Potters an office for Martin, which I was now going to share. I would have to see about getting some keys cut. Martin had given me one to his office but not the back entrance.

"You can go up in front of me; I'm not having you stare at my arse." I did as I was told. At the top of the stairs, she said she was going back to bed and would appreciate me not making any noise.

I unlocked the office and went in. Martin told me he never bothered to lock the filing cabinets, as anything of value would be placed in the safe. Not wishing to take the desk I cleared some space on a heavy pine table that sat under the window and then, extracting files on all the businesses, sat down at the table and started to read.

I almost leapt out of the chair. I had been so engrossed in the files when Amy popped her head round the door and asked, "Would you like a bacon sarnie and cup of tea? Sorry but I can't remember your name."

She was dressed now in a blue long sleeved blouse and a flowery skirt, and had applied some make up.

"It's Chas, and yes I'd love a buttie and cup of tea. Thanks very much."

"I'll give you a shout when its ready and you can join me in the kitchen." The smell of smoked bacon being fried pervaded the upstairs. My mouth was watering.

Ten minutes later, I joined her and Barry in the kitchen. Barry was still in his dressing gown and explained that normally he did not rise until ten o'clock. Sundays to Fridays, they closed at eleven and after a hot drink Amy would go to bed and he would clear the bar, which usually meant he got to bed at twelve thirty. Amy normally got up at nine to let the cleaner in and then unlock at ten. Saturdays they took it, as it came, and the pub never opened before twelve on Sundays.

"But you don't run this on your own do you?" I asked.

"No," Barry replied, and then smiled, "I've got two local lasses come in. Only part time, one each night, then both on Fridays and Saturdays. And of course there's Kevin our chef, and three girls who serve and help out in the kitchen. Other than Kevin, they're all part time. What exactly are you doing, it's not like Martin to give his office keys to strangers."

"I've known Martin for years. He knows I'm interested in getting myself a pub and offered to let me have a butchers at his set up. I felt really flattered when he offered to help."

"Oh that's okay then, I thought you were my replacement and Martin had forgotten to tell me." He chuckled to himself.

I finished my second sandwich and tea, and after thanking Amy returned to the office. The consolidated balance sheet for the last two financial years also broke down the figures for the individual businesses. Even a quick glance showed that The Black Horse was not achieving the gross profit of the other pubs. Maybe this was the one Martin wished to me look at. I smiled at the name of Fat Dicks for the restaurant. The figures looked okay but I had nothing to compare them with. What surprised me was that Club OMG was shown as an investment in the balance sheet with income but no explanation. No the odd one out was The Black Horse.

I was jotting a few figures down on paper when Martin arrived.

"Morning Chas, you start early. I hope you're not expecting me to meet me this level of commitment, at least not at this time in the morning."

"You're the boss; you can set your own hours. If I'm going to earn my crust I need to get up to speed with your businesses. Couple of things spring to mind though before we go much further. First, what do we tell your other employees why I'm here? I've just told Barry and Amy that I'm thinking of entering the pub trade and you as an old friend offered to give me unrestricted access to your set up. Secondly, I couldn't work out the balance sheet figures for Club OMG. It's only shown as an investment on the consolidation."

"The consolidated accounts are basically my personal position for the group and for tax. Club OMG is a different set up. I own the majority share of the business but when I purchased it, I was stretched and the bank wouldn't lend me any more money. I could see real potential for it and searched for a new lender. No one wanted to know. I had a word with one or friends, and then one day I was approached by a company called Offshore Business Financing Ltd. I'd never heard of them, but I met with one of the directors, Johny Johnson, and although I wasn't particularly happy with their offer, I took it. They didn't want to just lend me the money but wanted a share of the club. So far, I must admit they haven't caused any problems or interfered in any way. Johny was a nice bloke and occasionally popped in here for a pint and bite to eat. Haven't seen him for a few months now, but when he's next in, I'll introduce you. I did have a clause inserted that I could buy back their forty per cent plus a premium any time."

I made a few notes and tried to take in what Martin had said. "Do you have a set of figures for it? Just so that I have a complete picture for the whole group."

"I've got a copy at home; I'll bring them in for you. I don't have a problem with the club though; Zac the manager, and Errol, do a damn good job running it. Not a bad idea of yours to let it be known that you're only here to pick up a few ideas for running your own business. I'll go along with that. I thought I'd show you the other pubs today and get you sorted with a set of wheels, unless you have something else in mind."

"No, but tomorrow afternoon I'm down the physio clinic again. If it's all the same with you I'd rather we didn't visit The Black Horse. I'd like to go on my own and watch to see if I can spot anything going on. If they know I'm a friend of yours they won't say or do anything."

"Fair enough, I can see where you're coming from. I'd rather it was just an anomaly with The Black Horse, and not any fiddling being carried out by Pat and Jan."

That left just The Red Lion on the Wokingham Road, just outside of Reading, and The Woodman on the A30 just along from Hook, towards Camberley. Like the other pubs in the group, they were well run with food on offer.

Chas took me to a BMW dealer, where, after looking at a series 3 model, I decided that it was far better than my present Vauxhall that was seven years old and past its best. Even when I asked for leather, Martin never baulked. The added advantage was that it was automatic and saved using my injured left leg for the clutch. I was hesitant over the price but Martin claimed that the leasing deal was tax efficient for the business. Who was I to argue? Thanks to the recession, delivery would be about three weeks but in the meanwhile, the dealer was happy to let me have one of their demonstration vehicles.

Calling it a day, I drove off after reminding Martin to remember the balance sheet for Club OMG.

CHAPTER 7

Martin produced the accounts for Club OMG as promised. The blurb, at the beginning of the accounts showed that the accountants were Henshall Whyte, and that the company was owned by Martin and Offshore Business Financing Ltd., on a 60/40 split. The club showed a good profit and because Martin had picked up the property cheaply, due to the surrounding run down area, overheads were fairly low, and profit before tax was very healthy.

I put the balance sheet down and leant back in the chair. Sorting out the aggravation Martin was getting at the club and restaurant, was going to take time, and I would probably require some help. Best if I initially concentrated on The Black Horse, and why margins and turnover were lower than expected. I spent another hour comparing figures before my eyes were telling me they had had enough.

Decision made, I got out from behind my makeshift desk, and made my way to the car park, and the car the garage had kindly loaned me. The pub was the other side of Reading, in Caversham, and although I was not sure exactly where, I did not think it would take me long to find it.

Knowing the pub was on the Henley Road just outside of Caversham, I decided that it would be quicker to drive through Sonning rather than Reading. It took me forty minutes to reach my destination. The building was of a rather plain red brick construction although there was some ivy growing up a sidewall and which was encroaching along the left hand side at the front.

I looked at my watch. Ten minutes before midday. Sitting in the car, I tried to determine how my scrutiny should be approached. Still not sure, I picked up a copy of the *Sun* from the passenger seat and got out of the car. Entering the pub, through the entrance which was almost centre of the building, it led me in to a large bar area, with the bar placed along the right hand end wall. Close inspection showed there was a room about Twenty feet by thirty or forty feet which the left hand end of the bar jutted in to although at the moment there was roller shutter closing it off, and the room was unlit.

There were two men sat on bar stools when I entered and one of the pair got up and walked behind the bar. About mid to late forties, he was carrying excess weight around his middle that spilled over his belt. He had light brown hair, which was thinning over a round pale face.

"What can I get you sir?" He smiled showing discoloured teeth. Heavy smoker I guessed, by the cigarette he left burning in the ashtray, this side of the bar.

"Pint of ordinary please, and I'd like to order some food in a moment, if you have a menu."

"Certainly sir. I'll get your beer then find you a menu, although it is displayed on the board on the end wall."

"Oh yes, I didn't see it on the way in and by the way, the names Charlie." I hoped that by using Charlie, that if word got around that Martin had someone called Chas working with him, then, perhaps, the connection would not be made. I could have used Dave, Jim or any other name but I did not trust myself to respond if another name was used.

"Okay Charlie you grab a table and I'll bring your pint over. By the way I'm Pat."

I sat down close to the bar and turned to view the blackboard on the far wall. It was the usual pub fare of sandwiches, rolls and fast food meals. When Pat brought the pint over, I ordered a round of ham sandwiches with a side order of chips. Settling at the table with the bar to my left, I spread the newspaper I had brought with me on the table and hoped that I looked engrossed in what I was reading.

Three business types walked in while I was there. They took a table down the far end and sat deciding what to order. The fellow on the bar stool was a weaseley looking character in jogging bottoms, T-shirt and trainers. A shave would not have gone amiss. One of the suits went to the bar and gave his order for drinks and food. I watched as he paid in cash. Just less than four pounds were rung up for the drinks, and five pounds together with some change was put in a box at the side, that I assumed was for the food.

A bottle blonde-haired woman with bright red lipstick, and rather too much eye make up appeared with my food. About fifty she was wearing a white blouse with the buttons straining to keep the material together where it passed over her bust and where her waist should have been it moulded itself around a roll of fat. The ensemble was finished with black tights, flat shoes that looked more like slippers, and a tight black skirt just above the knee. Feeling kind, I judged the legs to be chubby rather than fat, and I guessed that she had never asked, does my bum look big in this, and if she had, then either someone was lying or she'd ignored the reply. She joined Pat and the customer at the bar, gave a raucous laugh and then disappeared to the back.

Pretending to look at my paper, I concentrated on listening to Pat and the customer at the bar. With my ability to overhear what was being said, reduced, by the occasional outbursts of laughter from the other end of the room, I managed to glean the fellows name was Andy and they were discussing a darts match to take place that evening. Nothing of real interest but I determined to return later. Pat got up from his stool and went back round the bar and drew them both another pint. No money in the till I noticed. I got up and went back to the bar for another pint.

"Thanks Pat and if you like I'll settle my bill please. It'll save troubling you again."

Pat took the money I proffered and rang two separate amounts in to the till and brought me over the change, which I waved away. He put this in a pint mug next to the box at the side of the till. I carried my pint back to my table and returned to my paper.

A couple entered the bar and took a table. Pat called out to the kitchen and the bottle blonde appeared and went to serve them. Before she had finished an old gentleman had taken another table and she saw to him as well. Two lads in BT overalls now stood between me and Andy, so listening in was impossible. This time I really did read my newspaper.

Nursing my pint, I sat there for another twenty-five minutes, then I picked up my empty glass, returned it to the bar and said goodbye. Both Pat and Andy acknowledged my leaving. Sitting in the car, I reflected on the box at the side of the till. If that was the fiddle, then I could not see how it would make that much difference and in any case, all drinks were rung up on the till. There had to be something else, all I had to do was find it. I decided I would go home have a quick forty winks, then give it some more thought.

CHAPTER 8

I was half way through changing in to a pair of Levis and a denim shirt when Martin called. I told him where I had been at lunchtime but not what I had seen. He would learn about that when I was sure of the facts.

"Chas, I had a chat with a salesman today and I'm having a mobile fitted in my car. You can also take it with you when you go anywhere else such as indoors, a pub, even the loo. I've phoned the dealers about your new wheels and they can have a kit fitted as a factory option, so I've told them to go ahead. Hope you don't mind."

"No." I replied, "It'll be another toy to play with and act nonchalant when I'm in a pub and I get a call on it."

Martin laughed. "A few hundred quid just so you can look casual and cool when it rings. Know what you mean, I love the thought of it."

"To be serious for a minute, do you mind if I ask some of my old colleagues for a bit of help if I need it? I won't divulge any more than necessary and I'll only ask those people I can trust."

"I don't have a problem with that. You may have only worked for me for a couple of weeks Chas but I trust your judgement. Within reason you have a free hand on this, you're the detective, do what you consider is needed."

"Thanks, and I won't let you down. I'm going over The Black Horse tonight on a little surveillance exercise. Hopefully I'll learn something."

"Okay, best of luck. I'm taking Jenny out tonight. You will have met her all those years ago when that drug business took place. She worked as a barmaid for me then. I used to be able to play the field then, but I daren't put a foot out of place now, she'd skewer my balls and spit roast 'em in front of me."

"Tall, slim, brunette, yeah I remember as do probably half the coppers on that case. Lovely lady."

"She is that, and she's kept me on the straight and narrow ever since we got together. Well, I'll leave you to it Chas, and best of luck."

He rang off and I continued getting ready. The phone rang again. Nothing important, just my bank telephoning to ask if I wished to see a financial advisor to assess my financial position and my ongoing future requirements. I questioned the caller as to whether she knew how I was fixed at this moment in time and she meekly said she didn't. "Just so." I said and put the phone down.

I had another hour before I needed to leave for The Black Horse, so decided to fire up my PC and see what

I could find out about Offshore Business Financing Ltd. A search of Companies House showed that the company was owned by Offshore Business Ltd. That company was registered in the Cayman Islands. It was part owned by Brian Jonathan Johnson, together with Offshore Business Ltd, on a split shareholding. Johnson owned five per cent. I do not profess to know a lot about the Cayman Islands, except, they consist of three islands in the western Caribbean and were a former British Territory. The banking system and tax regime was legendary for not disclosing anything. I spent forty minutes searching various sites but could find no more information. I needed to find some help to learn any more, or find Johnson and see what he could tell me.

The pub was busy when I got there with the side room occupied by what I took to be the home and away darts teams. The match had not started but the players were warming up. There was plenty of banter and leg pulling. The shutter was up on the bar that encroached in to the match room, and the till at that end of the bar was doing a roaring trade. Pat was looking after the darts players and a woman of about fifty was serving the rest of the bar. I managed to perch myself at the left hand end of the bar.

Pat turned towards me. "Back again then Charlie? What can I get you?"

"Pint of ordinary please, and a packet of nuts."

Pat fetched me a pint and the nuts, put the money through the till, and then hastily returned to the other end of the bar to tend to the darts players.

The evening was noisy with a large amount of barracking, although the match was taken seriously. Andy was there and appeared to be captain of the Black

Horse team. I could not watch what was happening in respect of the sales and cash all the time but I was quite certain that all sales were rung up and for the correct amount. By ten thirty, the match was over, The Black Horse having won, and I decided to call it a night. Whatever the fraud was, if there was one, had not shown itself tonight. I would be spending more time in The Black Horse.

※

"The boss wants that club wrecked tonight. He needs action, this has been going on too long. If you cannot do the job, then I will find someone who can. This is your last chance Rob."

"You were the one who told me not to get to heavy. Now you want to up the ante. I'll need more guys."

"Well you're the one who said getting a crew was no problem, so get them."

"They'll have to be from out of town and it will cost, probably another two or three grand. You'll also have to give me a few days to get it sorted."

"One now and two more if the jobs completed. Just get it done." The call terminated.

Rob thought about it then hit the speed dial on his phone. "Floros, who's calling?"

"Hey Floros its Rob. How you doing, you busy?"

"Rob, great to hear you again mate. I'm good, howsabout you? If you're phoning me you must want something."

"Well if you're not too busy I could do with a bit of help on a little job I've got on. There'd be a couple of big ones in it for you."

"What, where and when?"

Rob explained what was required and Floros agreed that he and two mates would be there on Saturday morning.

CHAPTER 9

On the Thursday evening, I decided to pop over to North Camp Farnborough to have a meal in a restaurant run by a Nepalese friend.

I enjoyed driving the Beemer; it made a nice change to my old banger. The evenings were drawing in now and it was dark when I reached North Camp.

Originally, Kumar Gurung was a Ghurkha based in the barracks at Church Crookham, but after serving his time, decided not to return home but open a Nepalese restaurant. If there was one thing the Gurkhas enjoyed it was a flutter in the casino, and whilst on attachment at Fleet nick I was tasked to look out for wrongdoing at the casino. I always thought that I had been chosen, as I was unknown in the area, but I learnt later that other officers found it boring and the job was passed to the new boy.

I had been spending most of my Thursday, Friday, and Saturday evenings outside the casino. Sometimes I ventured inside, but as most of the robberies and assaults had taken place outside, most of my time was expended, sat in my car. My luck was in one Friday night.

A group of soldiers had a successful night, and were celebrating their winnings. As my shift was almost over, I took a stroll around the car park, and then made my way to my car. I was still sat there when one of the group came out of the doors with a colleague, and began to cross the car park. They were walking between two cars when four lads of about eighteen appeared, blocking their route. Two other lads materialised behind the soldiers blocking their escape. Knowing trouble was about to kick off I jumped out the car grabbing my twelve and a half inch CID issued truncheon from the parcel shelf.

I made my way towards the gathering coming up behind them. Things were just beginning to start when I made my presence known. Startled the lads froze for a moment and in that time the two soldiers had struck out at the three in front of them seemingly unafraid of the staves that their aggressors wielded. I and the other two gang members watched mesmerized as the Gurkhas with one or two quick movements had the attackers weapons in their own hands and were dishing out summary justice.

I grabbed the other two, flashed my warrant card and told them to stay put. I shouted to the two Gurkhas to stop as I could see the lads had taken enough. They turned back to me and stepped over. Before I could stop them one had backhanded one lout while his mate sunk his fist in to the others stomach.

If I had not placed myself between them, I hate to think what would have happened. I asked one of the

Gurkhas to go back to the casino and request them to phone for a police van for prisoners. It was nearly fifteen minutes before the van and two uniforms appeared, and a panda car and a further two officers, a couple of minutes later.

Whilst we had been waiting, I learnt the two solders were Kumar Gurung and Gagan Rai. Their rank was havildar (sergeant) and naik (corporal) respectively. Initially they did not wish to press charges, but after a little chat with them, during which I explained the reason I was in the casino. Their colonel had requested police action, after a number of his soldiers were assaulted outside the casino, especially after winning.

Prior to coming to trial I met sergeant Gurung and corporal Rai a number of times and with their help managed to get three of the defendants a short prison term and the other three suspended sentences. They had also asked for forty seven other offences to be taken in to account. It was unfortunate that I had not seen the two Gurkhas strike the two lads at the scene of the crime, or they might have had a case against the soldiers. One of the three managed a shorter sentence, after giving up their collaborator in the casino. He was to be tried and sentenced at a later date.

Sergeant Gurung, who told me to call him Ken, treated me to an evening in the sergeant's mess, and we also met on odd occasions, where he introduced me to Nepalese dining.

Tonight he was sat with a group of young soldiers and there was a lot of talking and laughter going on. I had finished my starter of *momo* when instead of my waiter, Ken arrived with my *Piro Jhinge Machha* with *sag aloo* and *naan bread.*

He placed the food on the hot plate and I stood to shake his hand. "Nice to see you again Ken. I don't expect the boss to serve me when I come to eat."

"You will always get top service in my restaurant Chas. Sorry I couldn't come over earlier but I was sitting with my sister's son and his friends. They are doing a tour of guard duty at Sandhurst. If you wish you can join us, I will ask Razu to lay an extra place and bring your food over."

"No Ken, I don't want to impose on your family get together. But it's very kind of you to ask."

"Rubbish! You will be welcome. It was the boy's birthday last week and this is his first chance to sit with me. He has heard of you and the help you gave me and Gagan, he will be honoured to meet you."

By now, Ken had beckoned Razu over and asked him to move me to his table. It would have been an insult to refuse.

Ken introduced me to Asan, his nephew, and his friends Sunil, Bijay, and Suraj, as the man who helped him and Gagan Rai outside the casino.

"Your uncle exaggerates," I explained. "I did very little except watch three men armed with staves and knives wish they had stayed at home."

The banter continued, and although Ken's English was good his compatriots wasn't quite up to his standard although I learnt that although they were enjoying their time in Church Crookham, they found it a little boring in their evenings off. Why, I do not know, but I told them that if they went to the club on Saturday I would get them admitted with free drinks all evening. I only hoped Martin would not mind.

Friday morning I popped in to The Potters to pick up a copy of The Black Horse accounts to study over the weekend. Must have been my lucky day because Amy was making Barry a fried egg sandwich and was kind enough fry me one, with a cup of tea as well.

Martin called in just before eleven and I discussed The Black Horse with him. I told him on the face of it I could not see too much wrong, but was going out again this lunchtime to see if anything occurred. He wished me good luck.

I thought it politic to mention my invitation to Asan and his friends to visit the club on Saturday.

"I've offered to pay for their drinks for the evening. Asan's uncle has always treated me very well when I've eaten in his restaurant and it would be nice to do something for him in return."

"Perfectly okay," replied Martin. "The drinks will be on the house, you don't need to pick up the tab. There are a few private booths upstairs, overlooking the dance floor, I'll get Zac to reserve one for you and to alert Errol on the door that you'll be there. I've never had Nepalese food, what's it like?"

"Very much like Indian really. Many of the dishes are similar. I'll take you there if you want. Just name the day."

"I'd like that. We'll sort it out next week. Now, what do you suggest we do about The Black Horse. Am I just imagining there is something wrong there? I know there's a recession on and many businesses have lost twenty-five per cent of their earnings and we've got unemployment of seven per cent. It just appears odd that the pub seems to be struggling."

I nodded. "We could do a lunch and discuss whatever I learn in the meantime. As you say, it does seem odd that the figures do not tally with like to like. Unless you have anything else to add, I think I'll get on over there, and see how Pat and Jan are doing."

"No, you get off. I have the payroll to sort out and I'm hoping Amy has fish pie on the menu. You want to be here one Friday and try it. I'll see you next week."

The drive to Caversham was uneventful and as the lunchtime trade was well under way, the pub was quite busy. I took a seat at the bar. Andy was sat on the next stool, but today he was clean shaven and smartly dressed. I nodded a welcome.

"Charlie wasn't it? I think that's what you said the other day."

"Yeah." I replied, "Sorry but we weren't introduced the other day. Let me get you a drink."

"Thanks very much. I'll have another pint. The names Andy."

While we were talking Pat appeared. He picked up a pint glass and pointed at the ordinary bitter pump and I motioned yes. Two pints appeared. "Cheers Charlie, right kind of you."

"Nothing worse than drinking alone. Are you a local? Only I noticed you the other day and on the darts night."

"Fairly local I live down in the centre of Caversham, in Donkin Hill. Been using this pub for years. I knew Pat before, when he had a bar down in Reading. Nice couple him and Jan. They kept me on an even keel when my missus buggered off with some flash tow rag. By the time I'd paid her off, I was close to being destitute. Pat and Jan let me move in with them for a year or so until

I got straightened out. Still that's all water under the bridge now. How about you, are you local?"

"No I'm here on business. I sell stationery and we are sorting out a large contract with an insurance company. I'll be here for another week yet. Maybe even longer, because a chap I ran in to a couple of days ago is also interested in what we can offer. What about you, how do you earn a crust?"

"Working for the local brewery. Basically, I'm a rep. Lucky really, I've got a good portfolio of customers and am able to make a reasonable living. Are you staying local?"

"I'm in the French Horn at Sonning. Nice place but I prefer a pub atmosphere and I find pubs more relaxing. How did you fare at the darts?"

"We won, but not by much. I enjoy it for the company. We usually have a match every three or four weeks, as long as it does not interfere with the live music night. There's one in a week or so. If you're here you should come along."

All the time I had been chatting with Andy, I carefully watched the till. A couple of times money was not rung up on the till and the cash was placed in the box at the side of the till. The amounts were only small though. The sums that were placed in the beer mug I accepted as being tips.

Pat came over to join us and pulled another three pints. Nothing passed through the till.

"Busy lunch time?" I asked.

"Busy enough to make the missus complain about not having enough help in the kitchen. How are you anyway, been seeing a fair bit of you lately?"

"I just explained to Andy that I'm staying in the French Horn but I prefer pubs to hotels."

"Oh well, there loss is my gain. If you want to eat today you'd better be quick, the missus will close the kitchen in a moment."

I told Pat I was okay and that I would be eating later that evening. The chatter continued until Pat called time. He put a further half in to mine and Andy's glass then proceeded to collect empties. Finishing my drink I left the bar with Andy still ensconced on his stool. I returned to my car. I had sat there for a few minutes when Pat and Andy emerged from the back of the pub and strode over to a Montego estate car.

Arriving late at the pub, I was situated at the far side of the car park and, either they had not seen me, or they ignored my presence.

The back hatch was flipped open and the pair extracted a barrel, which they then carried to the rear of the pub. A few minutes later, they were back for a second one. The car was locked and they and the barrel disappeared.

I went back to the office but Martin had gone. Maybe what I required would be in one of the cabinets. However, my search was to no avail. Other than files for the balance sheets of each establishment, plus numerous correspondence files, and the payroll and employee files, the drawers were empty, except for the bottom one which contained an old pair of shoes and some manky Christmas decorations.

Deciding that Friday afternoon was not the best time to trouble Martin on an idea that may well prove fruitless, I decided to visit my mother, who I had not seen for a week or so since returning to work.

CHAPTER 10

Dawn had broken a couple of hours ago, but I was hardly ready for the day. I had spent the late afternoon and most of the evening keeping my mother company. She was only in her early seventies but suffered cruelly with arthritis. Mobility was a real problem and she needed the assistance of carers three times a day. We had a lot to catch up on and following my injury, she had been used to seeing me three or four times a week. Her body may have been weak but her mind was still strong or appeared to be. Her memory was not as good as it used to be, and she occasionally spoke rubbish.

Three carers had called whilst I was there. The first, a young Lithuanian lady who prepared her some tea and made her comfortable. Two more, a young blonde woman and an older woman, appeared later in the evening and changed her and got her in to bed. I made myself scarce during this visit. I would have done almost anything for my mum, but I drew the line at dressing, undressing, and attending bodily functions. I marvelled at how these women could do it all day long every day and maintain such a pleasant manner.

I had sat in a chair talking with my mother until after ten o'clock and she had fallen asleep, before making my way home to my own bed.

I yawned, sat up on the edge of the bed and grabbed some briefs off the chair alongside. Not bothering with any other clothes I went along to the bathroom, brushed my teeth and splashed water on my face. I went downstairs to the kitchen and put the kettle on to boil. I was in dire need of a cup of tea.

Finishing my second cup I glanced out of the window. It was going to be a fine day once the sun had burnt the dew off the grass, so I made a decision to mow the lawn. First though I had to pop to the local Tesco and get some groceries. Ahead of anything else though, a shower, and getting dressed was the order of things.

Later with the groceries packed away and the grass cut, it registered that my thoughts of a lazy weekend were pie in the sky. I had to meet Kumar and his nephew and friends.

It was eight thirty when we gathered at the club and I introduced my party to the two fellows on the door. As good as his word they knew to expect us and called Zac to let him know we had arrived. He arrived with Errol who showed us upstairs to a private booth, which was big enough for a dozen guests. He explained we were welcome to use the bar, but if we pressed the bell push, discreetly hidden under the table, a waitress would take our order and fetch the drinks. He pressed the button and a moment later a young woman he introduced as Maddie entered. She took our order and left.

Errol went on to say, "You'll have the same waitress all night and although anything you order will be on the house, you will need to tip Maddie. Twenty quid should cover it."

At this stage, I guessed my age was beginning to show because I had to lean closer to Errol to hear what he was saying above the music. It was deafening and the beat of the bass was bouncing off my chest. My fellow guests were enjoying it I noticed.

Maddie reappeared, Errol left us, and we sat down to enjoy our beers. Looking over the balcony, the place was only about half full, but Errol had remarked that about ten thirty it would get really busy and crowded.

A few drinks and two hours later I was beginning to regret my invitation to Kumar. My head was now bouncing to the beat of the music and my brain was warning me that tomorrow morning would not be a pleasant experience. Downstairs the floor was packed with heaving bodies mimicking the mating rituals of animals in the jungle. There was only myself and Kumar in the booth, the others having joined the throng on the dance floor.

Kumar looked at me, then leant over and shouted in my ear, "I have been involved in quieter wars than this."

I laughed and nodded my head not bothering to make myself heard over the incessant noise. We contented ourselves with watching Asan and his friends from the balcony. Mesmerised by the blare of music, I jumped when Kumar touched my arm.

He put his mouth close to my ear. "I think you ought to warn your friend, but maybe there will be some trouble. There are some men down there who have that manner about them. Look over there at the end of the bar, there are three there and others not far away."

I looked where he pointed and yes, there was a little group of men who had the image of seeking trouble. I pressed the bell push and moments later Maddie entered. I told her to find Zac or Errol and let them know what we surmised was about to happen. Just then, Asan came in to the booth to say he had noticed the little group who had already given him and his friends the evil eye. Zac walked in and told us to get the others up here and sit tight. Asan shouted something in my ear. He told us that Errol had already spotted the likelihood for trouble, and had a couple of his guys keeping a close eye on the group of potential troublemakers.

"Zac." I called. "Warn Errol and his guys that if anything kicks off Asan and his friends will be alongside them. They are not the enemy."

"Best they stay out of it," he replied.

"Unfortunately honour prevents them from doing so. Don't worry they are well able to look after themselves."

He shrugged and left muttering something about bloody amateurs. He then reappeared at the door. "On your own heads be it. I take no responsibility if any of you get hurt." The door closed and he was gone.

Kumar rose from his seat and peered over the balcony. "It does not look good down there Chas. I must go and be with Asan." Against my better judgement, I got up to join him. "No Chas you do not need to come. This is not your fight. I will be fine."

Just at that moment there was a crash and the sound of girls screaming. We both rushed for the door and stairs to the dance floor. Once downstairs there were people milling about everywhere. Some trying to get out, others seemingly intent on joining the melee. Over by the bar, the security guys were struggling to contain a group smashing furniture and throwing glasses or any other convenient object at those still caught up on the dance area.

A group of about ten louts were holding off six of Errol's men. You could see the flash of light off knives with others holding clubs fashioned from broken tables or chairs. A couple of the hooligans were trying to set light to some debris they had heaped together. There was space behind the good guys and I could see Errol giving them orders to hold firm. I then noticed just off to one side, out of Errol's vision, a swarthy looking yob, of possibly Mediterranean extraction. Not involved in the stand off, he was holding a piece of wooden chair leg in his hand and was indicating to the yobs that he wanted them to move forward and attack. I saw Kumar making his way toward him. I had not even realised he had stolen away.

There was movement from the rabble to Errol's left and I noticed one of the security lads take a beating to the head and collapse to the ground. Then there was sudden movement and with in a minute or so it was all over. I could hardly believe what I had just witnessed. Asan and his three friends had unexpectedly rushed the louts, disarmed them and dropped them to the floor with blows to what I could only assume were vulnerable points of the body. Errol's fellows waded in to secure their prisoners. Four men had defeated a group of ten in less time than I could tie my shoelaces.

By this time, an awful lot of the patrons had vacated the floor and were stood well back or had left the building. The swarthy man could not be seen, but I heard yelling from the toilet corridor.

Making my way over, there was the man being held against the door with Kumar guarding him. On closer inspection I saw the mans fingers were trapped in the doorjamb which was having pressure applied by Kumar.

Reaching him I said, "Who sent you?"

A torrent of abuse followed.

"Let me ask him." Kumar smiled and I had a nasty feeling that I could hear bones cracking as even more pressure was applied to the door. The scream was horrendous and brought Errol hurrying over.

"For Christ's sake, don't damage him the police will be here in a moment."

"Kumar's grin widened. "I just need an answer to my question which in two ticks this man will give me." The scream rose again as more pressure was added to the door and for good measure I leant against it.

"Okay. Okay. The guy you have over their in striped jacket and green trousers. He paid us. His names Rob but I don't know who pays him."

Kumar gave him a short, sharp jab to his solar plexus and he slid down the door until he was hanging by the fingers which were still trapped. Kumar let go the door and he fell groaning to the floor.

"Quick," I commanded, "Before any police arrive we need to know who sent him."

The three of us moved over to the group now sat on the floor. Errol went to pick up the one called Rob.

"Leave him Errol. You do not need to be implicated in this. Let Kumar and Asan find the answer." I placed a hand on his arm to restrain him.

With that, Kumar and Asan grabbed Rob and pulled him behind the bar and out of sight. A short shriek followed by some groaning, and then I heard Kumar say, "Well done. See it was easy, and you will still be able to father children." Being unable to walk they pulled Rob over to his friends.

With perfect timing, Zac joined us with a dozen or more uniformed officers. As they collected the yobs I heard a sergeant say, "There are two or three here that had better go straight to the hospitable. There's an ambulance outside". He instructed two officers to accompany them.

Zac and Errol joined me. I looked for Kumar, Asan and comrades but they had vanished in to thin air. Errol looked at me, smiled and winked. "I took them out the back way and showed them how to avoid the police by jumping over the gardens, down the street."

Zac whispered in to my ear. "I told them to go and not get mixed up in this."

"But what about the CCTV?"

"I've swapped the disc for a blank. Silly me I forgot to set the record button this evening."

As a copper, I would have considered no CCTV as bullshit, but unless you could prove otherwise, you had to accept it.

"Well done, but they'll still question you about them."

"I know, problem is they all look alike to me! Only problem I see is that one of us has to phone Martin and tell him what's happened."

"I'll do it in the morning. I do not see the need to bother him tonight. He's probably in bed by now. The damage is superficial, so won't take much to fix." I laughed. "Not like that poor blokes fingers."

I waited to have my name and address taken and told the officer that I would make a statement although I was only a bystander. It was late and I wanted to get home to bed and it now occurred to me I was probably over the limit to drive home. I had a word with Zac and he arranged for a taxi.

CHAPTER 11

Sunday morning was not good. Although I had not expected too, I slept like a log after getting back from the club, not waking until it was gone half past nine.

Gathering my thoughts I realised I had to let Martin know of last nights debacle. His mood was ebullient when he answered but had dampened slightly after I had described last night's events.

"Well at least that's the end of that," he declared.

"I don't think so Martin. We may have stopped last nights attack but those yobs were only hired help. Whoever it is will find plenty more to replace them. Still the one named Rob gave us a name to go on. I'll put a few calls in to old colleagues and see if they can put a face to the name."

"Whatever you say. Lucky those friends of yours were there. By the way, how's your hip? Any twinges?"

"Only the usual aches and pains. I was a bystander last night, no action. If that's all Martin I need to get ready for lunch with my neighbours. He was a colleague of mine for a while, until I was invalided out. Nice couple but he's a bit of a stickler. You know, Twelve thirty is twelve thirty not twelve twenty nine, nor twelve thirty one! Probably why he stayed with uniforms. She's nice though. When I first came home from hospital she used to pop round with casseroles and just keep an eye on me." I rang off.

I showered, shaved, and made up my mind that after lunch I would return home and have the Sunday day of rest that I had envisaged twenty-four hours earlier.

Monday morning I tried the old number I had for Wendy Johnson. It went to an answering machine so I left a message and gave my mobile number. I then called Martin and told him what I had been looking for Friday afternoon and had forgotten to ask about yesterday when we spoke. The answer was all old paperwork was in boxes in his garage at home. The more recent book work would be with the accountants. Unfortunately, he had been remiss in labelling all the boxes and unless I was lucky, it might take me a while to find what I was looking for.

Martin was off to London but Jenny would be at home and show me where the boxes were stored.

I drove over to his house, a large detached house of five bedrooms, a large games room and indoor pool. I stopped at the large wrought iron gates, pressed the intercom and waited for Jenny to answer and let me through. There was a short straight drive that then formed a circle in front of the house. There were well kept gardens, with the lawns looking immaculate. Martin had said his relaxation was mowing the lawns at the weekend. Unlike my hover mower, Martin had a ride-on with gang mowers. There must have been two or three acres and I knew there was a paddock out the back. I walked up the steps to the front door and rang the bell. I wouldn't have been surprised to find the door opened by a butler.

Jenny may have been a few years older than when I first met her but she was still that same attractive, vivacious, brunette.

She looked me up and down. "You still look the same as when I met you on that drug business in Marty's bar. Marty told me you'd be calling so I've made some coffee. You've never been here before have you? We'll have coffee then I'll show you around. Come in, don't mind the dog he don't bite but he'll leave you covered in dog hairs. Still they'll come off with a bit of sticky tape."

Her chatter was incessant and her voice reminded me of the ditzy blonde Aimi MacDonald, off the television. I followed her in and through to a kitchen that was enormous. She told me to sit on a high stool while she busied herself with a fancy coffee maker.

Coffee and the grand tour over, she finally took me through the utility room to the garage. Like the rest of the property, it was not small. There was parking for three cars, plus a large ride on mower. The roof space was open for half then boarded to make like a mezzanine floor with steps leading up.

"They're up there whatever it is you want. Will you be all right on your own? I'm going to nip down the shop. Ham roll okay for your lunch?"

I butted in. "You don't have to bother getting me a lunch. I'm perfectly fine."

"Nonsense, Marty wouldn't forgive me if I didn't look after you. See you in a while," and with that she pressed a button and one of the up and over doors began to rise. She hopped in to an XJS drophead, started the engine, reversed and then sped off down the drive.

I climbed to the loft area to begin my search, with no idea where to begin. About two thirds of what I guessed was well over forty boxes, were marked with name of the pub and some did at least have a date on the outside. Thirty minutes later I gathered that the date on the box or even the pub name was not entirely accurate. I was engrossed in yet another box when the soft purring of the Jaguar's V12 engine made its way in to the garage and parked. Jenny got out with a carrier bag that seemed almost empty.

"Sorry I was so long but I met a friend and she wouldn't stop talking." I looked down at her. "Give me ten minutes then come through to the kitchen and have lunch with me."

I must admit that the dry dusty atmosphere of the loft space had made my throat dry and lunch and a chance to stretch out was welcoming. I finished the box I was on, then made my through to the kitchen.

"Sit down and tuck in. I've made tea and am just waiting for it to brew. My dad used to say if the spoon won't stand up in it, then it's not strong enough. Do you like the ham; I get it from a local butcher. He boils and slices his own. It's not like that wet, thin sliced rubbish, that supermarkets sell. You had any luck with those boxes? Marty told me why you were here. I told him to watch the till at the pub. When I worked in one pub the landlord would take the money for a pint but ring up five pence for a box of matches. He then placed a penny piece on the shelf. At the end of the night he counted the pennies and that gave him the number of pints that he could pocket the cash for. Got real upset one night when I was short of copper and scooped them all off the shelf and put them in the till. Lecherous old bastard used to wait for me to bend over for the bottom shelf or look down my blouse. I'm sure he used to dribble."

She paused for breath and I laughed. "Yeah, I can see you would have that effect on men. The young officers that were with me on that drug case never stopped talking about you but I don't think any one of them had the courage to ask you out."

She giggled. "Oh! To think I may have been a coppers wife. Eat that other roll up, I never eat much at lunchtime. Just a crispbread or something."

We chatted while I ate my roll, or to be more exact Jenny kept up an unrelenting stream of idle chatter. "Bloody hell," I thought, "how does Marty live with this." I stood up and took my plate over to the sink, then returned to the garage.

After fifteen minutes I got lucky. In an unmarked box were rolls of paper and a quick look showed they were from the Black Horse. Hopefully, the answer was at hand. I carried the box to my car, and after saying goodbye to Jenny, I drove back to The Potters.

※

Settling myself in to the office chair I telephoned Zac.

The aftermath of the fracas on Saturday night had been cleared up and decorators were repairing the damage where they had tried to start a fire. The leader known as Rob was also picked out in the security tapes of previous attacks. Zac was sure the police did not believe that he did not know who the Ghurkhas were, but were not pushing for the truth.

Ringing off I then called the number I had for Wendy. Again, it was an answering machine and I left another message.

My next call was to the accountants, asking if I could have the till rolls and daily and weekly financial sheets for The Black Horse, for the last three months. They promised to send them the following day.

Making the decision that I was going to have an early finish, I picked up my car keys and left for home.

CHAPTER 12

I was watching the Monday night football on Sky when the telephone rang. It was Wendy returning my calls. We went through the usual pleasantries and I brought her up to date with my new job and then she asked what it was I was really after.

"If you feel uncomfortable, or do not wish to involve yourself then I require nothing, but if you are able to help then I need a little information. Nothing sinister, but I need to know what or who I am up against." I told her the story finishing at Saturday night.

"So what is the problem? Are you implicated in any way?" she asked.

"No, I just stood and watched. I know nothing about this Budgie character and I don't want to wade in and find I'm out of my depth. Being shot once in your life is still one time too many!"

She laughed. "Well thanks to you rescuing me and leaving the force, I got the promotion to fill the empty sergeant's slot. Give us some details and I'll see what we've got. What name do you have?"

"Budgie, that's all I know, but he should have appeared on the radar at Surrey and Hants."

"That's all you've got. Budgie! Still as you say, a search will reveal all if he's known to us. I'll give you a ring in the next day or so."

Exchanging promises to get together at some time, in the future the call ended.

The next morning I spread the paper I had collected from Martins over the table, the floor, the sideboard and any other space I found available. I just knew the answer lay there in front of me. I studied dates and figures for nearly three hours and was close to concluding that maybe the answer was not in front of me. Time for coffee and a bite to eat. Thirty minutes later, I laid all the lists in date order. Day to day, week to week, month to month, there was nothing that stood out. If I had been Greek I would have yelled *eureka,* of course nothing stood out, it was not there, but the answer was in front of me. I would be more sure when I had the up to date figures from the accountants. I telephoned Martin.

Later that afternoon Wendy called with information regarding the character Budgie. Firstly, his real name was Arthur Lee and he had form for breaking and entering, malicious damage, GBH, and was suspected of arson. Additionally he was also suspected of being involved in the suspicious death of Jimmy Briggs, Maggs old boss. An unpleasant individual by all accounts, arrests for violence were abundant and even an arrest for murder, although the charge was later dropped. He was a known associate of a Billy Maggs.

Budgie carried out the dirty side of Maggs business. Maggs had a few minor charges against his name, but nothing substantial, although Wendy said the feeling was, he was implicated in a gang war, and the death of an adversary a few years previously. He had kept his nose clean for a few years, and although rumour still had it he was involved in escort agencies and massage parlours, with a dose of protection thrown in for good measure. One or two of the girls he employed had remarked that he had a cruel and vicious side to him, and was not averse to giving them a beating. Outwardly, he was a respected businessman and property developer.

"Chas if you know something, then let me know, but for Christ's sake don't get involved, you'll be fighting well above your weight."

"Thanks Wendy, but I don't intend to get involved as you say. I reckon pressure is being put on my boss, although neither he nor I can work out why at the moment. Thanks for that. I owe you one, and if anything comes of this, then I will give you the heads up."

I rang off. So, Budgie was just the muscle for Maggs. Why would he wish to harm the club, I needed to find out. I left a message on Martin's mobile for him to call me.

Martin called after forty minutes. "Sorry Chas but I was involved in some business talk with the bank. How can I help."

"What do you know about your partners in the club?"

"Not an enormous amount, I dealt with a chap called Johny Johnson. I have his number if it's any help. Pleasant enough old chap, although he does ramble on a bit."

I made a note of the number and after a few pleasantries rang off. I called the number Martin had given me, and it was picked by a lady after a few rings. "Farnham double six two nine four three, can I help you?"

"I hope so, I'm looking for Johny Johnson, have I got the right number?"

"Yes you have the right number. Wait just a moment and I will get him for you. Who shall I say is calling?"

"He doesn't know me, but my names Chas Barker." I could hear the sound of somebody coming down some stairs and then their footfall as they walked on a hard floor.

The receiver was picked up and a voice said, "Johny here. Can I help you? I'm afraid your name doesn't mean a thing to me."

I explained who I was and what it concerned.

"I don't have an awful lot to do with Offshore Business Financing any more. I still have a small holding of shares, but that's only because it suits the owner. I receive a small dividend every year which covers my golf club membership, and that's about it. Why is there a problem?"

"No." I lied, "but I'm thinking of investing in a club in Camberley and noticed your company was a shareholder. I was wondering if you'd be interested in selling. I could make a reasonable offer."

"Maybe, but unfortunately I'm the wrong man to be talking to. The man you want is Billy Maggs. I'm unable to give you his number but I will telephone him and ask him to call you."

Maggs! The name Wendy had mentioned. Small world sprang to mind. "Thank you that would be most helpful." I gave him a wrong number.

CHAPTER 13

Wednesday was wet and miserable. I had to report to the hospital at nine thirty for some physiotherapy, and to have the consultant check that everything was as it should be.

It was, and the consultant told me that unless anything occurred there was no need for further visits, except an annual visit.

Good news but it had taken nearly two and a half hours to get it. Never mind, with any luck I would not be going back again. I got in the car and set off for The Black Horse.

When I got there, Pat was serving behind the bar, with Andy perched on his usual stool. Jan was serving at table.

I took the stool next to Andy. "Hi there." I greeted, "would you like that topped up?"

"Hello Charlie, haven't seen you for a couple of days. Found a better pub?"

"No. It's just that my boss popped down at the weekend to go over a few things. Spent the last couple of days making sure everything was up straight." Pat joined us and I ordered a round of bacon sandwiches.

"You in tomorrow night. Gotta live band in the back room, well not actually a band but three lads and a bird, who make a bloody racket. Still it gets the younger crowd in. Should be a good crowd."

"I'll see. I'm not sure yet what the gods have in mind for me."

We chatted for a while and I had my lunch, and another drink, then I made my excuses and left.

Once back at the office I telephoned Martin and brought him up to date with what was happening at the Black Horse. Nothing more I could do for now so I turned my mind to the problem at the club.

I flicked through the telephone directory until I found I found an estate agent and land agent in Camberley. They were an independent company. A young woman answered the telephone and I asked if they had anybody in their office that could talk to me about the properties in York Street. She told me the senior partner was the best person to talk to and she would find out if he was free. A few moments later, he came on the telephone.

"Good afternoon. I'm John Calder. I'm sorry, but my young lady in the office didn't give me your name."

"My fault I never gave it to her. I'm Chas Barker. You may not be able to help, but I'm interested in some properties just off Princess Way, in York Street."

"I know the area; it's only a short walk from this office. What exactly is your interest and enquiry?"

"Well I passed through Camberley the other day and spotted the street which looked fairly derelict. To me it looks ripe for development. Is it council owned or private?"

"Until a short while ago most of it was private but nearly half was owned by a developer. Over the last year a few more of the private properties have also been snapped up but I cannot tell you who by. No planning permission has been sought, so I assume it's all speculative. We've acted in some of the cases; I'll get my secretary to bring in the file." The line went silent for a moment. He came back to tell me his secretary would only be a few minutes, and then he may be able to give me more information.

He continued. "You may well find you're too late to buy now, as on the QT, I have heard that the remaining owners have been approached by agents acting for some company, and they are offering a not unreasonable price." There was a tap on the door and a young woman stepped in and placed a file on his desk. He opened it and scanned quickly through the papers. "Here we are. I thought I was right. One or two of these properties are owned by a company called WM Developers Ltd., although most are owned by a multi national. I'm afraid I can't tell you much more than that. You could try Companies House, or search on the properties at the Land Registry to try to discover more."

I thanked him for his time and spent a moment deciding what to do next. I phoned my solicitor and asked her how I could make a search at Companies House. According to her, it was a very simple process and if I gave her the details she would get one off in tonight's post. I gave her the information and asked for balance sheets, directors and shareholders. Next, I asked her if I could discover who owned the properties in York Street. Again, she promised to get it underway by close of business.

Now all I had to do was wait.

CHAPTER 14

Thursday turned in to a lazy day. I was kicking my heels until Marion, my solicitor, came through with the results of her searches at Companies House and the Land Registry.

I did not have guilty feelings, as I was conscious of the fact that I would be working tonight. The telephone began ringing. It was Martin.

"Just wanted to confirm that you were going over The Black Horse tonight, only I thought I might pop over."

I was alarmed. "What! I'm hoping to finally provide you with my conclusions on why the turnover doesn't tally with what is seen from the other pubs in the group. If you show up he could well cover up any wrongdoing. Please Martin don't ruin any outcome by making your presence known."

Okay. Okay. Don't get all het up. I won't do anything to damage your plans. What are they anyway."

"I'll tell you when I have a result."

"Fair enough, pull this off and I'll give you a small share in the business. That sound okay?"

"Sure, but you don't have to do that, I've only been with you five minutes."

"So you have, but there's method in my madness. Jenny has been on at me for over a year now to spend more time with her and Tara. She moans that whenever school holidays come along, I'm not around. Whines on that we've never even had a family holiday together. Deep down I know she's right, so now I'm doing something about it."

"We'll talk about it later, Martin, that's a big step for both of us to take. And another thing, I didn't even know you had a daughter."

I heard him laugh as he put the telephone down. "What the hell was that all about." I thought to myself.

Having plenty of time on my hands, I called in on my mother on the way to the pub. I made her a cup of tea and we chatted about my new job. I did not mention the fracas at the club, as she still could not understand why I had left the police force. I stayed until her carers came to put her to bed, then made my excuses and left.

The pub was heaving when I arrived and the band was making a good show of an Eagles number. Pushing my way through to the bar, I squeezed in beside Andy. We greeted and I brought us both a pint.

"They're not bad." I spoke loudly to be heard above the music.

"They mainly perform older stuff. Most bands do covers these days, but they do write and perform their own stuff every now and again.

Barrel of Lies

There were three lads, two on guitar and a keyboard player. In such a small place it could have been deafening but they managed to keep the noise to a low roar. There was girl on the lead guitar and she followed their rendition of *Hotel California* with a Bonnie Tyler track. I along with many others could not help but join in with *It's a Heartache*. The temporary bar at the end was going well and when Pat turned and waved, I acknowledged.

There was break during which the toilets developed a queue and the bars became frantic.

Andy tapped me on the shoulder. "Bloody clever how by use of the keyboard and a bit of electronic wizardry you can do away with the drums."

"Just as well." I answered. "There'd hardly be room in there for a full set."

I felt someone touch my arm. I turned and a young woman said "Hello again. Didn't expect to see you here."

I looked again and saw it was the carers, the two blonde women, I'd seen at my mothers earlier. "Let me get you a drink." Having spun the story I was staying in the area I hoped they would not say anything to alert Andy to my deception. They asked for an orange juice and a white wine. The drinks seemed to take an age to arrive but thankfully the conversation was restricted to how good they thought the band were. The young blonde one, thanked me for the drinks. The band retook the stage and she and her friend said they should rejoin their friends in the side room.

Andy punched me in the side. "You're a dark horse. Where did they come from?"

Thinking quickly I replied. "Met them in the car park when I arrived. They'd dropped their car keys and I helped them look for them. Didn't even get their names."

Further conversation ceased as the Charlie Rich hit, *The Most Beautiful Girl*, hushed the room. Standing on the bar rail to gain extra height, I pulled a disposable camera from my pocket and took a couple of pictures picture through the bar to the side room. I indicated to Andy I was going round to get a better one and he should watch my pint and hold on to my stool.

"You taking pictures of them? Bloody hell they ain't that famous. Still, if they ever hit the big time, you can sell them to some magazine or other."

Returning I asked Andy if he knew whether they had any cassettes with their recordings on. He did not think so. The evening continued and although I was working, I still found time to enjoy the performance. On the way home, I came to the conclusion that it had been an enjoyable and hopefully successful evening.

CHAPTER 15

It was pouring with rain next morning and there was a chill wind blowing. I had not drunk a great deal the previous night, but my head was banging. I needed aspirin and coffee.

The paperwork from The Black Horse was still spread over the dining table. It had been useful but nothing conclusive so I put it all back in the box, then took it out to the garage and placed it in the car boot.

I grabbed my raincoat and an umbrella and picked up the throwaway camera and my car keys. I drove to The Potters and parked up. Grabbing my coat and brolly, and the box of tally rolls, I went up to the office. Barry was preparing the bar for lunchtime opening.

"Morning Barry, you gotta few minutes you could spare me?"

"Sure Chas. Give us a couple of minutes and I'll come up to the office. Would you like a coffee? Amy has just loaded the Cona machine so there'll be one handy, I'm having one, I'll bring you one up."

I'd already had an overdose of caffeine this morning but a drop more would not hurt. I was making room in the cabinet for the box of papers when Barry appeared with two mugs of coffee.

"What is it I can help you with/" enquired Barry.

"Quite simple really. I'm trying to work out how the accountancy side of this business works. Martin says he doesn't get involved, he pays accountants to look after the figures. Having been to his house to try to find information, I can confirm that that he's absolutely right. Accountancy is a complete anathema to him. Tell me what you do with till figures, you know the tally rolls."

"As you said quite simple really. At the end of each day the breakdown of figures from the till are entered on to a sheet provided by the accountant. You know, beer sales, wine, spirits food, mixers, and cigarettes. Every sale made is entered in the till under a code. When the till is totalled it sub totals the various sales then provides a grand total. The next bit is the difficult bit. The cash, cheques and card sales have to agree with the total. Rarely does. Sometimes the difference is easy to spot, other times its impossible. At the end of each month the sheet together with the tally rolls are collected by Martin and he delivers them to the accountant. That's about it."

"Thanks Barry, that's really helpful. Do you enter every single day down separately on the accounts sheet?" He confirmed that. "Is the fish pie on today, if so I'll be down to the bar later. I've got to nip down the town first."

He laughed. "Yeah, its Friday, so the fish pie will be on. If you're not back in time I'll make sure Amy saves you a dishful."

The rain had stopped so I decided to walk in to town, and to the local Boots, to get the pictures I had taken last night developed. The results were just what I needed.

After enjoying my lunch of fish pie and a spotted dick pudding, I returned to the office and telephoned Martin. I needed him to action the final part of my plan.

CHAPTER 16

Monday and Tuesday were quiet but on Wednesday, Martin produced the paperwork I required and my solicitor called to say she had the search from Her Majesty's Land Registry in front of her. It did not explain much but she said she would now search on the title numbers they had provided. I thanked her and she told me she was happy to help, especially as I was paying for it.

I arranged with Martin that we would meet at my house to evaluate the information I had gathered on The Black Horse. He agreed it was pretty damning and he would be pleased to see it.

"You say that after the last punters had left the premises on Thursday night that the guy you know as Andy was still there and the lights remained on in the bar until gone twelve thirty. When you looked through the window they were playing with the bar till."

We resolved that we would visit the pub next Thursday and confront Pat with our findings.

"Do you know what pisses me off about this Chas." I shook my head. "I interviewed and employed the bastard. Why? He gets a good salary and bonus. Still, that's not your problem. Okay one down one to go. How are you getting on with the club."

"Very little to report, at least until Marion, that's my solicitor, comes up with information, and that may take a while yet."

"Make sure you claim her bill from the business. Solicitors never do anything cheap. What I said the other day, sort this out and you'll deserve your share in this business."

"Well as you raised the subject, I'd . . ."

Martin interrupted. "Not going to discuss it now. I need to be off. If I don't see you before, I'll see you Thursday." And with that he grabbed his car keys and was gone.

That was not the first time he had raised the issue of a share in the business, but he always avoided discussing the matter. Irritating, but as I was not overly concerned about a share of the business, I pushed it to the back of my mind.

I called in at The Black Horse a couple of times over the next week, and on the Thursday evening arrived early. The visiting darts team, from The Red Lion, were not due until seven forty five, and Pat was setting up the side room bar, aided by Andy.

The opposing team arrived and suddenly the bar got busy. As usual Pat ran the side room bar with Jan and a barmaid running the normal bar.

The evening progressed and I began to wonder what had happened to Martin. I did not feel it was my place to broach the subject of fraud with Pat.

As the match was winding up and people were beginning to go on their way a bearded fellow tapped me on the shoulder. "Good match wasn't it mate. Thought your lot were lucky to win."

I turned and stared. "Your right it wasn't a bad match at all,"

He looked straight at me. "Chas you fool, don't you recognise me?" The voice had changed and I immediately recognised the weirdo as Martin. "Bloody good disguise. Jenny done it for me. I walked in with the blokes from Red Lion, so I was hardly noticed. I've watched nearly all evening, Pat running that second till. I still can't work out though how he does it because the barrelage is roughly in line with the takings. If he was selling my beer and keeping the money it would show."

"But that's what I told you. It's not your beer or spirits."

Whilst we'd been talking the bar had emptied apart from Pat and Andy. Pat came over. "Sorry Charlie but I shall have ask you and your friend to drink up. Its been a busy night and I need to close up."

"Sorry Pat. We'll be on our way."

Martin and I went out to my car and sat watching for a while. I had parked by a window and although we could see in, it was not that clear. Martin got out of the car and peered in through the window. He must have watched for twenty minutes, and then climbed back in the car.

"Well I think I've seen enough Chas. If we meet back here tomorrow morning at say ten o' clock, then we'll see what Pat has to say."

"Hold on another few minutes Martin and I'll show you why the books balance. I'll just reverse over there in the shadows, out of sight."

We sat there for ten minutes before Andy appeared with cask that he loaded in to his car, together with a case of bottles. He left the tailgate open and went back inside.

Moving quickly I reached in to the glove box, and grabbed a disposable camera. Striding purposefully over to Andy's car, I took a couple of pictures of the contents of the boot. Hearing voices I hastily retreated to my car and knelt down out of sight. A few more bits and pieces were placed in Andy's car, and then he and Pat said a few words and then parted company.

When all was quiet, Martin went back to his car and we both drove away.

CHAPTER 17

"I don't care what this tosser, Charlie, or whatever his name is says, there are no fiddles going on here. Check the stock, check the till rolls, and check the banking. Everything is accounted for."

"Oh, I know everything tally's up. It's not my stock or cash that's short, it's the rent."

"What rent? I don't owe any rent."

"Fifty pound per night for use of side room. Two hundred a night for selling alcohol from my bar. Over say two years at say thirty nights a year. That's fifteen grand, then there's loss of sales say another fifteen grand, and that's just a ball park figure."

Pat's face had dropped. "But I never took anything and at the end of the evening I used to ring up extra sales. You made money from it."

"Pat you have no idea do you. You're employed to sell my beer, my wine, my spirits and my mixers. Not set up a private bar in my premises. All the money that went through the second till was made on my premises. Yes you rang a few extra drinks through my till, but then all sales should have been put through my till."

"What proof have you got of all this? The only stuff in this pub is what belongs here."

I had kept quiet until now, but butted in. "Pat I have photographs, I have watched you run the bar from the side room and the amount of money that passes through the till. I've seen Andy deliver beer from his car in advance of any match or music night. I and Martin watched last night as the two of you tidied up, I took photographs of the stuff, as you put it, loaded in to Andy's car."

Martin added. "And I've spoken to the director at the brewery and a quick look over their records shows the number of casks of beer that Andy has claimed as sweeteners for his clients. He's as deep in the shit as you over this. I don't think that by five o'clock tonight he will still have a job at the brewery."

More words were bandied but in the end Pat accepted he was finished. Martin wanted them gone by three that afternoon or he would involve the police. Pat pleaded for more time, but Martin was adamant that they were gone that day. Whilst all this was going on a chap called Ian arrived and after a quick chat with Martin, began to set up for lunchtime opening.

Ian was about seventy years old and had managed pubs for Martin until he retired. Now he covered holidays, sickness, or events such as this, when required. He came with a wife, Jacquie, who would cover the kitchen.

I left Martin to deal with the remaining aftermath of the morning's event and headed back to the office.

The solicitor had come back with some answers to my questions.

As John Calder had informed me, most of the properties were owned by a well-known public company, but WM developers Ltd owned five.

The only interesting fact in the search was the name of the sole director. William Maggs. I had no doubt that this would turn out to be Billy Maggs, Budgies boss. I would have a word with Martin when he came in. Meanwhile I would have a chat with the planning office and see if development was on the cards.

The officer at the council explained he could not provide full details, but the council was looking at modernisation of the whole area. It was envisaged that shops, offices, and flats would be built. The council were looking at private money to finance the project as there own coffers were empty. The matter was to be discussed at a meeting in three months time.

Martin arrived two hours later and we considered the information now at hand. Martin then telephoned his bank and arranged to meet with his manager the next morning. He suggested I went along with him, as at some time in the future I may have to deal with the bank on my own. Whilst we were sat there, we heard a car engine roar then the sound of gravel being thrown up in the car park. This was followed by Amy shouting, up the stairs, that we needed to go down and look at my car.

My, or should I say the dealers car had a dent in the bonnet where a can of pink paint had landed before spreading itself over the bonnet, screen and roof. It had then run down over other panels.

"I saw the bastard that did that. He was in a green Montego estate car. I've got the number too." Barry looked pleased with himself.

He deflated slightly when I said, "Thanks Barry but I have a very good idea who the culprit is." I looked at Martin. "Well do I telephone the police?"

"Got to Chas, it's not our car and the dealers won't be very happy when they see this. Serves the bugger right, I didn't involve the police this morning because him and Pat were going to cough up five grand and I said I'd let it go, but we can't overlook this."

I was stuck there for another two hours waiting for the police to arrive and take a statement. The dealership was very good over the whole affair, and arrived with a replacement car, and arranged for the freshly painted model to be taken away.

The next morning I met Martin at the bank in the town. Discussion took over an hour but after a cursory valuation of the pubs, club and restaurant the business manager arrived at a figure, which he considered would meet the approval of his senior manager. He promised to phone at lunchtime to advise Martin if he had agreement in principle.

As soon as we were back at the office, Martin telephoned his solicitor and asked him to give notice to Offshore Business Financing Ltd that he intended to purchase their share as laid out in the loan agreement.

I left him to it as I had to go the local police station and make a statement regarding the paint job on my loan car.

CHAPTER 18

Four days later Martin received a telephone call from Johny Johnson who informed him that his fellow director did not accept his proposal and was demanding that Martin should sell Offshore Business Financing Ltd the remaining sixty per cent of the club.

"Johny your friend doesn't understand, I have the legal right to purchase whereas he doesn't. Tell him he either enters in to this arrangement or I will arrange a private hearing in chambers to ratify the position."

Martin could hear an exasperated Johny on the other end of the telephone. "I'm sure he understands he just does not agree with it and I feel I ought to tell you he is not a man to cross as I have found to my cost."

"Just tell him he has fourteen days to come back with a figure."

"I'll tell him but he won't like it."

Martin put the receiver down. "You heard that did you Chas?"

I grinned. "Yeah I heard. I think someone is a little miffed. This should draw the unknown director in to the open. I know we have our suspicions but this will confirm them. From what we know of these characters, we should watch our backs."

"Why? Do you think it will get rough?"

"Well, I don't think he'll take this lying down. Look just keep your eyes open and be aware. This man has some nasty friends."

"Okay. Okay, I'll take care."

Four nights later Martin pulled up to his gates. He cursed the remote for not opening the gates, as they remained firmly shut. Lowering his window, he pressed the code in to the keypad at the side of the drive but this had no affect either. Cursing and muttering obscenities to himself, he climbed out of the car to inspect the gates. He was up close to them before he spotted the wire bound round the bottom. Bending over to unravel it, he heard a sound behind him.

"Mister Bishop. How nice to meet you. We need to have a little chat."

Martin stood and turned. "Who are you and what do you want?"

"Me? I'm nobody that you'd want to know. I'm only a messenger. I'm here to help you with your business decisions. You know the one where you sell your sixty per cent of Club OMG to the other shareholder."

"That ain't likely to happen. You can . . . ."

Martin never finished his sentence as a fist exploded into his midriff. He doubled over gasping for air.

"Wrong answer Mister Bishop. Now let's try again. Repeat after me, I will arrange to sell my holding in the club to my fellow shareholder."

"Never."

With that a further blow landed on Martin's nose causing blood to flow copiously. Martin fell to the ground and a kick to his ribs followed All Martin saw was a smart shoe with a silver buckle raise itself for another strike.

Barking and a woman's voice could be heard. The attacker stopped his attack and walked up to the gate. "Get lost or I'll phone the police." The dog continued to bark and act threateningly. Torchlight flashed across the assailants face. "I can see your face and I won't forget it, so piss off."

The man stared at her for a moment. Martin found a fist sized piece of stone that edged the drive and moved behind his aggressor and brought it down hard on the back of his head. Unfortunately his own injuries had sapped his strength and the blow did little more than gash the attackers skull causing blood to flow. For his trouble he received a further fist in his solar plexus, before the man turned and hurried away.

Jenny spoke through the gate." Are you all right. Why won't theses stupid gates open?"

In a nasal voice Martin panted, "They're tied at the bottom. You might need some shears or something. I'll be alright here go and get something to cut that wire."

Jenny began to trot back to the house. She reappeared five minutes later with a pair of pruning shears. Try as she might, Jenny could not cut the wire.

Blood still dripping from his nose, Martin told her to give him the cutters. It took a few attempts but he managed to remove the wire. "Lock the car." He said, "I'll move it in the morning. I don't want to get blood all over the interior." He winced as he stepped through the gates.

"You need to go to the hospital Marty. I'll clean you up a bit then drive you down to casualty. I reckon you've got a broken nose and a couple of cracked ribs."

Martin knew better than to protest.

CHAPTER 19

"Bloody hell Martin, what the hell happened to you?"

"Be careful you said. I should have listened. Some cretin jumped me last night." Martin went on to explain what had happened.

"Why do you think I told you to keep your eyes skinned? Wendy told me this pair had a history of violence. We've rattled Maggs with this option to purchase and he will not take it lying down. Do you know who the attacker was or could you pick his face out of some mugshots?"

"If I can't Jenny can. Better than that, the stone I clobbered him with, Jenny put in a plastic bag because it had some of his skin and blood on it. Watches too many cop programmes. Told me it was forensic evidence. Blood type and so on. Two o'clock before the police left last night, and the senior bloke drank half my bottle of scotch. It's not that I'm scared for myself 'cos I bloody well am, but its Jenny I'm frightened for"

"Clever girl. She's dead right about forensics but it's too risky for her to remain here. Get her away from here Martin. Send her on a holiday, or let her stay with her mother or a friend. Just get her out of the way. And you can move in with me for the while."

"I'll try but she was dead set against it last night and this morning. Stubborn bitch when she wants to be. The problem is, she thinks it's me being a worry guts. You phone and reason with her, she might accept it from you."

I did and after a serious chat and a little coercion, she agreed to go that afternoon to stay with a friend. She explained that she could not leave immediately as the police were with her taking a statement and showing her some mugshots. No, she had not seen anyone who looked like the attacker. Martin and I left the office to drive to his place so that he could say goodbye to Jenny and pick up some bits and pieces for his stay with me.

Later Jenny drove off to stay in Derby with an old friend whilst Martin and I returned to the office.

Martin telephoned his solicitor to let him know what had happened and to press for action regarding the transfer of shares.

I perused some of the copy documents that Martin produced. Mostly legalese, it was difficult for a layman to understand. I would take it home and have another go later.

Things were quiet for a while and then ten days later Martin had a telephone call asking him to meet at the club. On his own, which the caller stated meant no one not even solicitors. Arrangements were made for two days time at two o'clock. Despite my objections,

Martin impressed upon me that he meant to carry out the instructions and go on his own.

I arrived at the club at one fifteen and spoke with Errol who I had arranged to meet there. Maggs could not object to that, after all it was Errol's place of work. They could always ask him to make himself scarce.

I had parked the other side of the street so that I could keep an eye on the club entrance, but would be far enough away so as not to be noticeable. Just after one thirty, a Mercedes entered the street and cruised slowly down the street. I lay down low across the passenger seat so as not to be noticed. It passed me again twice more, the driver peering intently as he passed. Lucky for me there were half a dozen other cars parked. It was cheaper than the three pounds a day to use the municipal car park. On its fourth pass it pulled in and stopped outside the club. A short man who had to be Maggs got out the rear passenger door. Dressed in a navy camel coat he tugged the coat cuffs to pull the sleeves down. He then surprised me by walking a few paces down the street and producing a key from his coat pocket. He used this to unlock and enter one of the empty properties. The driver, who I assumed to be Arthur Lee a.k.a. Budgie remained in the car.

A couple of minutes before two o'clock I saw Martin's car enter the street, then park two cars up from the Mercedes. Lee quickly exited the car and watched Martin. He was wearing a black bomber jacket and black leather gloves. As Martin locked his car and turned back towards the club, Lee moved beside him, pressed what I took to be a gun in his side, and walked him to the property that Maggs had gone in. They entered and the door slammed shut behind them.

God bless mobile telephones. I called Errol first, informed him what had gone down, and suggested he go to the back of the house four down from the club and hide in the back garden. Next, I called Wendy and told her what I had seen.

Reaching the house and kneeling by the door, I jammed the letterbox open with a scrap of timber and listened.

Maggs was talking. "Now we're alone and not likely to be disturbed, let's discuss the transfer of your shares to Offshore Business Financing, shall we?"

"It's not going to happen. I am taking legal proceedings to forcibly purchase the shares I don't own."

"No mister Bishop. It's you who doesn't understand." Shouted Maggs. "You will sign those shares over to me and sooner rather than later. I have all the documents here with me. They only require your signature and then we're done."

"Never. In a few weeks time the courts will have declared me the legal owner. Why don't you just . . . ."

Martin never finished as Maggs indicated to Lee that he should intervene. Lee transferred the gun from his right hand to the left. A solid punch was delivered to Martin's stomach and he doubled over and sank to his knees, only to receive a kick in the ribs. With the damage from his previous beating not yet healed the pain was excruciating. Lee dragged him to his feet and sat him on an old rickety dining chair. "Do you want me to tickle him again boss?"

"Only if he's not ready to sign. Let's ask him. Are you Bishop, ready to sign?"

"Get lost, I'll never sign."

Lee looked at his boss, who nodded to him. Lee held the gun out for Maggs to take, then used both hands to lift him to his feet. He then punched him again. Martin collapsed to the floor and Lee rained kicks at him.

"Stop you fool. He's no bloody good unconscious." Maggs intervened.

Lee grabbed Martin and dragged him back to the chair. Maggs moved in front of him and snarled, "We can keep this up all night if need be. Now are you going to sign these forms or not? I am not playing around and I don't intend to leave here until this has been sorted." Maggs backhanded him across his mouth.

Groaning with pain, talking through a split, and bleeding lip Martin croaked. "Admit it Maggs, you've lost. I won't sign your damn forms and I'm no use to you dead. You will never gain control of the club."

Maggs began to laugh. "Idiot! Do you think I have no other means of persuading you? How about the lovely Jenny? We're only three hours or so away from Derby, I'm sure she'd like to meet Budgie again. She upset him the other night appearing as she did. Oh and don't think your no use to me dead. Did your solicitor not mention to you the almost standard clause in the contract. It says that in the event of the death of either party that the surviving shareholder has the right to purchase the other's shares at an agreed value so that he is not saddled working with a new director who may not have the same views the direction the company should take."

Martin winced and his shoulders slumped.

Maggs carried on. "Of course your untimely death may lead to a complication which is why I am being generous and offering you the easy way out. I'll give you a few minutes to consider what I have just told you."

This was a turn for the worse and I quickly made my way back to the car to ring Wendy. I needed help and urgently. Call made I returned to the door. I wanted to warn Errol of the fact that they were armed, but other than walking the long way round, had no means of communication.

"Well mister Bishop have you mulled over your options? Budgie is hoping that you'll want him to meet the wife."

Whether Martin had passed out I did not know, but no reply was forthcoming. I heard Maggs tell Lee to get some water and rouse him.

All was quiet for a while and then I heard Maggs telling Martin that time was running out and if he wished to save his wife, then he should sign on the dotted line. I could not hear if there was any reply. Maggs started shouting again, and then there was silence. A loud bang from a gun being discharged caused me to leap back from the door.

"Christ Almighty Wendy where the bloody hell are you?" I muttered to myself. I moved back to the door and was so intent on listening for sounds inside, that I almost jumped out of my skin, when a hand on my shoulder startled me.

"Move back to the safe area sir, just down there to the right. DS Johnson is waiting there for you." The words were quietly spoken by an officer in bulletproof vest, helmet, and visor. As I stood he said, "We'll deal with this now." He beckoned behind him and a further two officers stepped forward, carrying an enforcer to open the door.

"You need to do something. Didn't you hear the gunshot? Christ Almighty, he could have shot him."

"We heard it sir, and if you clear the area we will be able to action a rescue. Now please move back down there, to the right."

Joining Wendy in the designated safe area, I suddenly realised that Errol was at the rear of the building, where there were sure to be further armed officers. She quickly got on the radio to warn her colleagues.

There was a lot of radio traffic, but little action and I voiced my concern to Wendy.

A sudden crash as the front door gave way followed by a shout of, "Armed police. Put your weapons down and come out one at a time with your hands raised." Any sound from inside was muted.

Maggs and Lee froze for a moment or two then Lee made a bolt for the back door. Maggs was a lot slower and an armed officer entered the room with the order for Maggs to drop the gun he was holding. Maggs, not realising he was holding the gun, was nonplussed for a moment or two. The command to drop the weapon was repeated and Maggs complied. Doing as instructed he spread-eagled himself on the floor, and with his arms pulled behind his back, was cuffed.

As Lee rushed through the rear door he took a step or two up the overgrown path before Errol hit him behind his knees with a piece of timber he had found in the garden. Although it broke in two, it was sufficient to cause him to stumble and fall forward. Errol leapt on his back and pinned him down. Although Lee was a large powerful man, Errol was no slouch and struggle as he might, Lee could not dislodge him.

The scuffle was still in progress when a voice told them to pack it in. It came from a figure dressed in riot gear complete with helmet and visor and accompanied by an officer in stab vest and holding a machine pistol. As Errol started to rise he was grasped by the arms, and a pair of cuffs were quickly slipped on to his wrists. A quick pat down showed he was not carrying any weapons. Another officer cuffed Lee, and checked him over.

"Hang on a minute," yelled Errol, "I'm on your side." He was ignored and told to proceed through the house. Out on to York Street Wendy came forward and told them to release Errol.

"Fine way of saying thank you for apprehending your prisoner," growled Errol. "If I hadn't been there he'd have been away."

Wendy looked at the officer who was unlocking the cuffs. "Is that right?"

Sheepishly the officer replied. "We were covering the wrong property. They all look the bloody same at the back."

An ambulance arrived and two paramedics rushed in to the property. It seemed like an age before Martin was carried out on a stretcher.

I went over to see how he was. There was blood on his face and the skin where it showed was deathly pale.

"Hang on in there mate, you're safe now." He returned my greeting with a pained smile, and croaked, "We'll see about the partnership when I get out."

CHAPTER 20

Wendy had joined me at The Potters for a lunch. The main topic of conversation was the arrest of Maggs and Lee the previous week.

"You would not believe the falling out between the two of them. At first, they both refused to speak but when it was pointed out that the only fingerprints on the gun belonged to Maggs and that the gun was the one that killed Jimmy Briggs, he began to talk. He named Lee as the killer. Lee, of course has implicated Maggs."

I smiled. "Must be a feather in your cap as well. I'm pleased they'll be going down for a long spell after the damage they done to Martin. He still hasn't contacted me since the attack, although Jenny has kept me informed."

"We did interview him at the hospital initially but when we called at his home a few days later, he was very withdrawn."

The conversation lingered on and the lunch finally ended at gone three o'clock. Wendy returned to the station and I went upstairs to the office to finish off the days work. I had been running the business with Barry's help. I telephoned Jenny every evening both to enquire how Martin was and to keep her up to speed with company business. She told me that as from next week she would come in to The Potters every day from eleven until two thirty to help out.

At the end of the following week, Jenny informed me that she and Martin were going to Florida for three weeks and she would be grateful if I would continue to hold the fort in the meanwhile.

For the next three weeks, I continued to keep the business ticking over, until Martin and Jenny returned from their break. Martin was still not fit enough to return to work. The physical injuries were almost mended. The problem was the mental scars he carried. Jenny popped in when she was able, and kept me up to date with any progress. A couple of months passed then to my surprise Jenny arrived early one morning with a stranger, who she informed me was interested in purchasing the pubs, restaurant and club.

I was stunned by this news, but thought it politic to wait until the stranger had gone, before asking for answers to questions that had now arisen. I made my excuses and left them to it.

Needing time to think things over, I drove over to see my mother who because of the extra workload, I had neglected of late.

The young blonde carer was there when I arrived, making my mother a cup of tea and some toast. I offered to do it if she wished to get away, but she pointed out that she could not reach her next client too early, as she had to dispense medicines. Chatting to her, while she busied herself, I asked if she had enjoyed the evening at The Black Horse. She had, so I told her I would leave some complimentary tickets for the club, which she and a friend could use.

The three of us sat there while my mum drank her tea and ate her toast. Leanne, which I learnt was the carer's name, sat with my mum, and myself, regaling us with stories of holidays etc. Christ, she made me feel old.

Later I drove back to the office to discover that Jenny and the stranger had left. Balance sheets and accounts were strewn over the desk together with various jottings.

The next day Jenny came in to the office to inform me that she and Martin were selling the business but that all jobs would be safeguarded. I cannot say that I was surprised, although it would have been nice to have heard it from Martin.

CHAPTER 21

Things moved very quickly over the next few weeks. The stranger who I discovered was called Owen Strong was a director of a pub company called Pub and Club Company Limited.

Jenny did have a chat with me and explained that Martin had lost all confidence and now wished to sell up and move to Florida. They were getting a very good price for the business. She told me it was enhanced because of the value of Club OMG, which was now part of a desirable development area.

He did however wish to see me and asked if I would call on him at home. Not having seen him for a number of weeks, I was surprised how gaunt and drawn he looked. He was no longer the self assured man that I knew and seemed nervous of everything around him. The meeting was short and Martin spent most of it repeatedly apologising for letting me down.

Owen Strong met with me and explained that they wished the group to continue as before and to assure me that all managers and staff jobs were secure. The purchase and hand over would take place in three weeks. In the meantime he would be grateful if I would visit every establishment and reassure the present incumbents that their jobs were safe and existing pay and bonuses would be honoured.

A week after the handover a familiar face appeared. Andy! Or to give him his full name Andrew John Strong. Brother of Owen.

"Mister Barker, how nice to meet you again. Isn't this fortuitous, at least it is for me."

"Well! Well! Andy. I won't say it's nice to see you again, because I'm basically an honest person. What can I do for you?"

"Nothing at all. It's what I can do for you. As from tomorrow you are free to do whatever you want."

"How come?"

"Well, having checked all the personnel files, the only person without a contract of employment is you."

My mind began to work overtime. He was right. With all that was happening, Martin and myself had never got around to drawing up and signing a contract. The look on Andy's face showed that he could see I realised where this was going. "I'll make it easy Andy. I'll go now." And with that I picked up one or two belongings from the desk and made to leave.

"Hold on a minute," said Andy, "What about your car keys?"

"Check the files again Andy, the car was purchased in my name and never transferred to the company. Supposed to be on a leasing agreement but another job we never got around to. Another little piece of paper that never got dealt with while we were so busy trying to trace the crooks involved in this business." Dangling the keys from my finger I walked out of the office.

I now needed to go home and think what I was going to do with the rest of my life. It took nearly six months for that decision to be made. I was going to buy my own pub.

CHAPTER 22

I had learnt a lot from working for Martin but not enough about the running of a bar and cellar. Before Jenny, Martin and Tara departed for Florida I sought his advice.

He looked a new man since I had last seen him, but not the old Martin I had worked with. He gave me a few pointers and suggested I contact the LVA, and get on a course to learn the art of keeping a good bar. Also employ a good bar and cellar man, who could do it all for me!

He still had regrets over what had happened to me and produced a contract of employment he had his solicitor prepare and date two months after my joining the business. He asked me to sign it and he would send it to the Strong brothers, apologising for not having sent it in before. He pointed out a clause that gave me twenty thousand pounds, should my employment be terminated. Oh how I would love to have seen the look on Andy's face when that appeared on his desk.

I spent the next year learning the trade and viewing pubs and restaurants which were for sale.

In May ninety-four, I found a nice pub in Yateley. The Old Bell. Not to far from home.

The premises consisted of a public bar, a saloon bar and a small room with an old fashioned bar billiard table and dartboard. There was a kitchen and office with a couple of storerooms. Downstairs was a cellar, which appeared free of damp. The upstairs accommodation was three bedrooms, a kitchen, toilet, bathroom and a large dining cum sitting room.

Although generally in good order, a fresh coat of paint would not go amiss. Outside was a good-sized car park. The present proprietor was about seventy years old and had run the pub with his wife for over thirty years. There was no hot food served unless you counted the steak and kidney pies that were only available Saturday lunchtimes. The rest of the time, it was crisps, nuts and cheese or ham rolls. Even though takings were good and often topped seven hundred and fifty a week. I reckoned I could improve on that. There was work to be done, I was up for that, but first I had to have my offer accepted.

The following Monday I called to see the owners, Bert and Alice, to make my offer. The occasion turned out to be fortuitous, although I did not know it at the time. My offer was twenty thousand less than the asking price of two hundred and fifty five thousand, but I argued that I would need to spend money on the décor. Turnover was for wet sales and the gross profit was just under sixty per cent.

My idea was to knock the public and lounge bar in to one, then by removing the walls to the storerooms and demolishing the wall between them and the games room annexe, I would finish up with one large bar and a restaurant able to take about twenty-five or so covers without being too crowded. With any luck I would be able to persuade a brewery to cough up some of the cash, or at the very least provide an interest free loan.

Alice seemed warm to the offer, but Bert said he would like a day or so to consider. I agreed that was only fair, and the business side of our meeting was put aside and we retired to the bar for a drink before evening opening.

Bert was pulling us both a pint when he groaned and the pain on his face was obvious. Heart attack, I had seen it before and rushed round the business side of the bar shouting at Alice to telephone for an ambulance. I reached Bert and checked his chest which although not pronounced was rising and falling. He was unconscious and I rolled him in to the recovery position. Alice put the telephone down, and confirmed an ambulance was on its way. I could see she was beginning to panic.

"Alice, Bert will be okay. He is breathing and I think he's beginning to regain consciousness. It's a good sign, now be an angel and pop upstairs and find me a pillow and blanket."

She did not move and I repeated myself only a little louder this time. Alice suddenly turned and hurried upstairs I breathed a sigh of relief. Although I had received the training, I had never had to perform CPR on a real person.

Bert was beginning to regain his consciousness, but was disorientated and agitated by this experience. I was relieved to hear a siren and a short while later a shout as a paramedic called out. An older man with a younger woman came in to the bar area carrying resuscitation equipment and a case of instruments and drugs. They commenced their life saving skills, while I reassured Alice. Within a short while Bert and Alice were on their way to Frimley Park Hospital.

Alice had pressed a bunch of keys in to my hand and asked me to take care until either she or her sister came to take over. I promised her that I would.

Her sister arrived thirty minutes later, in a taxi, and entered the premises with the aid of a walking frame. I was amazed. She must have been over eighty and I could see there was no way she would be able to run the bar.

She may have looked frail, but her voice was strong. "Hello. I'm Vera; you must be the Chas my sister mentioned." She looked me up and down.

"Pleased to meet you Vera. Alice told me her sister would be along to look after things, but excuse my asking are you intending to run this bar?"

"Young man, do I look as though I could work this bar. No. I intend to put a note of apology on the door and just stay here until Alice returns. I thought I would then stay with her for a few days. She told me she'd give me time to get here and then give me a call. All this just as they're trying to sell the place and take it easy."

"I know and I've just made them an offer although it hasn't been accepted yet. When Alice calls, ask her if she would like me to open up and run the pub until they are in a position to decide where to go. I don't want paying, but with you here to keep an eye on me and hopefully keep me topped up with tea and coffee, I'll be able to get some hands on experience of running a bar. What do you think?"

Vera eyed me quizzically. "Well I think you must be mad, but I'll ask our Alice when she calls. Meanwhile I'll let you get me a cup of tea."

Although she used a frame, Vera managed the stairs quite well, with me carrying the frame and her gripping the handrail. We sat in the kitchen, and after a little searching; I found the necessary bits and pieces to make the cup of tea.

Alice told me she had been a domestic science teacher, and when I looked bewildered, she explained they called it food technology now. She had never married, and in her younger days had helped behind the bar during school holidays.

It was gone four thirty when Alice called. To begin with, she made excuses for me not to run the pub, but after I took the handset from Vera and had a little chat with her, she agreed to give it go, for a few days. Bert was conscious and undergoing tests, and the outlook was very good. The doctors were hopeful of a full recovery, although surgery was necessary.

My first night as a temporary landlord went well, even if at times service was a little slow. I even managed to change a barrel! However, the locals were good-hearted about it once they had heard the news concerning Bert, which all things considered, allowed me to get away with the odd mistake. Fortune favoured me when a woman of about thirty-five who told me her name was Jane, offered to lend a hand if needed. Like me she did not require payment. She told me she had helped out when either Bert or Alice were under the weather. I told her I would have to ask Alice but if she agreed, I would be glad of the help. Alice knew Jane of old and was happy for her to chip in.

The next two weeks passed fairly quickly, with Alice spending most of her time at the hospital, but sparing a morning to help me with the order. Bert was progressing nicely and was expected to be allowed home, in a week or so, if his recuperation continued as expected. He would not however be fit for work.

CHAPTER 23

Bert was back home and complaining every minute about not being allowed in his own bar. I was still working everyday, alongside either Alice or Jane. Alice told me the break away from Bert's moaning was heaven sent.

I broached with Alice my offer and she asked if I would wait another week or so until Bert was more able. She did mention that she was happy with my offer, but Bert was hoping that because the asking price was realistic, that they would achieve it.

The next week, before I had the chance to sit with the two of them, the agent telephoned to say he had received an offer of five thousand below the asking price. Alice told me that if I could match that offer then they would sell to me in lieu of the unpaid work I had put in.

All things considered and having worked the pub and enjoyed my time with the locals, I agreed that I would match the offer. Alice told me they would let the agent know.

Alice had informed the agent of their decision and within the hour, the agent returned with news that the other interested party had increased their offer by twenty five thousand for a quick exchange and completion. Alice told me and I advised her that she should accept the offer.

She made many apologies and repeatedly told me she was sorry, but they could not afford to turn the extra money down. I reluctantly agreed.

The prospective purchaser wished to meet her and have a look at the premises on the Wednesday, and I told Alice I would make myself scarce on that morning. A visit to my mother was long overdue, as I had neglected her whilst running The Old Bell.

※

Mum was watching some terrible daytime television show when I arrived. I made her a cup of tea and found some chocolate biscuits in the cupboard. We settled down with our refreshments and mother told me all her news. Many items were repeated and sometimes she mixed up or forgot names and places. The doctor had called the previous day and passed her one hundred per cent fit but had added the proviso, for her age. She did however say she would arrange for a doctor from the Wokingham hospital to call and assess my mother's mental state.

I stayed until twelve thirty and the carer arrived. It was Leanne, and I thanked her for the kindness and consideration she showed my mother.

I drove back to my house, showered and then made myself a sandwich before driving back to Yateley. I would continue to help Bert and Alice if they still needed me, until their sale was completed.

Jane was serving behind the bar when I walked in and told me Alice was upstairs conferring with Bert, on the offer that had been made. I stayed on the customers side of the bar and asked Jane to pull me a pint.

"I wish it was you getting the pub," she said as she put the pint in front of me. "You get on well with the locals and I enjoy working with you."

"I think it's a pity too. I've loved my time here even though I wasn't being paid. Still the experience will stand me in good stead when I do get my own pub. There's plenty out there but not very many good ones, at least not ones with such attractive, charming bar staff."

She laughed. "Yeah and I'll miss the compliments even from you, you smooth talking old sod."

Jane went off to serve some other customers and I looked around thinking of my future plans for the place. I was reminiscing over the last couple of weeks when Both Bert and Alice appeared behind the bar. There were only eight or nine people in the bar, not including Jane and myself, and we all looked genuinely surprised to see Bert back behind the bar for the first time since his heart attack.

Bert banged a glass on the bar to attract everybody's attention. Not that he needed to, as every pair of eyes were upon him. "As you are all aware, myself and my good wife are hoping to retire, and I can tell you all now that we have accepted an offer for the pub. I will let you all know when the handover will take place. I can say no more at the moment until we've spoken with Chas who has kept this place going in my absence. We owe him a debt of gratitude and feel it only fair to discuss our decision with him. That's all I've got to say until Alice and I have spoken with Chas."

I looked at them both and smiled. "There's no debt Bert, I've enjoyed every minute I've spent behind this bar."

"Maybe so, but come upstairs and have a cup of tea. The quacks don't allow me anything stronger at the moment."

I moved behind the bar to the accompanying noise of clapping, to follow them up to their living quarters.

"The kettle has boiled." Alice said over her shoulder as she disappeared through to the kitchen.

I patted Bert on the shoulder, saying, "no regrets Bert, I meant what I said down in the bar. I've loved every minute here."

Alice came in with a tray loaded with teacups, plates and some biscuits.

She placed it on the table and Bert looked at her. "Go and bring that bottle from the fridge. I feel like a proper drink and bugger what the doctors say."

Alice once more went to the kitchen and returned with an ice bucket with a bottle of Krug chilling, together with three glasses.

Bert laughed. "Didn't I mention it, the pubs yours."

The expression *you could have knocked me over with a feather* never had a truer meaning. "What? But you've received a far better offer than I could make. Did they withdraw it?"

"No they actually increased it to tell you the truth. I'll let Alice tell you what happened."

Alice chuckled. "A man called Andrew came to inspect the premises and to confirm their offer. Everything was going well, and then he popped down to his car and brought up the bottle of champagne we're drinking. Bert and I were sat in here and Andrew asked if he could make a call to his partner. I told him to use the kitchen. He spoke with someone called Owen and I overheard him say something like, don't worry its in the bag, Barker won't be getting this one. He was sneering as he said it and he followed up with, I owe that bastard one."

Bert interrupted. "I told the missus to say nothing but to leave it to me. When he returned, I told him that you were willing to go to thirty thousand over the asking price, and that we had all but accepted the offer. He got a bit surly then and said why did we let him come all the way out here just to tell him that. He then phoned his partner again and said they would go to Fifty thousand, if we signed a letter of intention today. Forgive me, but I then told him we didn't like you that much, and found you a bit pushy. He responded by saying you had screwed him over before and we should be careful you didn't do it to us. That was when Alice used language that surprised even me, and told him, excuse my French, to fuck off." They both burst out laughing and it slowly dawned on me who Andrew was. Andy Strong my friend from the Black Horse.

Bert looked at me and smiled. "Are you happy to pay the asking price?"

"Of course. Of course," I replied. "I just can't believe all that I've just heard."

CHAPTER 24

Purchasing The Old Bell was the easy part. Trying to get planning permission for the addition of a conservatory, enlarged car park and other alterations was sheer hell. Finally, after nine months I was able to instruct a builder to commence work. It was agreed he would work one section of the pub at a time so as to minimise disruption and allow me to keep some form of cashflow. As a fillip to my customers I was selling my beer, wines and spirits cheap, in the hope they would not desert me once the renovation was complete and I increased prices.

Two months in to the build a stack of timber mysteriously caught fire, damaging the plastic frame of the conservatory. Although the police investigated, no person was ever found responsible, albeit I had my own thoughts concerning the culprit, or culprits guilty of this arson. It was not so much the cost, but the time delay it caused.

Minor irritations continued over the next few weeks causing further delay. Once again, the police were unable to find the guilty party. Irritations they were and I decided to take matters in to my own hands.

A quick search of Companies House found the Pub and Club Company Ltd and the names and addresses of the two directors and three shareholders. The two brothers and a company called MYOB Holdings Ltd. It took four days but I was serving in the bar and in walked Andy.

"You bastard! It was you who set the police on me wasn't it? You want fucking trouble then you got it."

I looked shocked. "Whoa, hold on there. I don't know what you're talking about. I'll admit I don't like you, but I have no idea what your problem is."

"Like hell you don't. My house has been turned upside down by your copper mates, and they won't even tell me what it was all about."

"Look I know nothing about police raids, where you live or anything else. I do however, feel that you are responsible for the run of bad luck my contractor has suffered and I dare say that you've pissed off more people than just me. I'm not surprised that something has come back and bitten you on the arse."

He looked at me as though he did not know whether to believe me or not, and then turned to leave.

As he reached the door I said loud enough for him to hear, "Oh, and if I suffer any more fires or materials being stolen, or deliveries of farmyard manure, then I know a friend who will plant child porn on your hard drive and tip off the vice squad."

He snarled and addressing the drinkers in the bar, "You all heard that. If anything happens and the . . . ."

In unison, the customers shouted, "We didn't hear a thing." I smiled at him. He walked out slamming the door shouting over his shoulder, "You aint heard the last of this you bastard."

Danny, one of the builders, who was having a lunchtime drink, asked, "Do you really know somebody who could plant kiddie porn on his computer and get him arrested?"

I winked. "No, but he doesn't know that."

There were no further incidents to delay my rebuilding programme.

CHAPTER 25

With the work finally finished, I now had one large bar, together with a restaurant that extended in to a conservatory and a brand new kitchen to service it. Jane helped me interview and choose some waiting staff, and a phone call to Fat Dicks and a chat with Laurence and Max, put me in touch with an accomplished chef, called Ben Jones. He agreed to help sort the kitchen out, together with any extra staff that may be required. I agreed that I would leave him to make the choices regarding the menu.

    Feeling in a generous mood, I invited all the locals who had stayed loyal, even if they were light users of the bar to enjoy a three-course meal of steak, fish or something vegetarian on the house. This number turned out to be thirty-three and by placing the tables in a square in the restaurant and a T shape in the conservatory, I could just get them and myself and two other guests fitted in. This left room for another half a dozen customers should any turn up. It was not quite free for I told them that there would be a charge of five pounds per head to cover the tip for the staff, with plentiful supplies of wine or beer provided. There were no detractors.

The evening got off to a flying start and although I had allowed for up to six extra guests, nine turned up. No worries and room was found for all, and by ten o'clock large quantities of wine and beer had been consumed. My special guests, Bert and Alice, were overjoyed at meeting with old friends again and were thoroughly enjoying themselves.

At ten fifteen the mood changed when there was a loud noise that I later learned was a shotgun, followed by the sound of glass shattering and my fellow revellers in the conservatory were showered with broken glass. Luckily, it was safety glass and there was no real harm done.

I and one or two others were quickly out of our seats and rushed outside, only to hear the roar of a motorcycle as it left the car park. I hurried back in to check that everybody was okay and told Jane to phone the police. They always say that if you want a quick response from the police then mention firearms. I can vouch that it works.

As luck would have it, the SIO (Senior Investigating Officer) was my old boss John Chivers, who had now reached the rank of Chief Inspector who turned up with Wendy Johnson. There were floodlights in the car park and plods were crawling on hands and knees searching for clues. Other than the rubber laid down when the motorcycle tore out of the car park there was nothing.

"Well Chas, who have you been upsetting now? Amateurs don't discharge shotguns 'cos they know the aggravation it can bring them. Any ideas?" John asked.

"None whatsoever. I did have a spot of bother during rebuilding, but I doubt if they had anything to do with this."

"And who are they?" enquired John.

I explained what had gone on before and Wendy said she would make a few enquiries and see if anybody's cage was rattled.

She called me a few days later and told me her enquiries had come to nothing.

"They told me that you would explain that they are steering well clear of you. In any case, they both had alibis for the time of the attack. They're on camera in their own club. Have you put the frighteners on them?"

"Not really. I put a scare in to Andy and I'm sure that it was enough to deter any further interference by him or his brother. I must admit that other than a few scrotes who I helped put away, I can't think of anyone."

We chatted for a while then Wendy got up to leave. "Chas if you think of anything that would help please let me know. Every time you and guns are in the mix there is trouble."

I laughed but looking back she was right.

CHAPTER 26

A few days later, everything was back to normal. Well, except for the workmen repairing the glass in the conservatory. I had been able to seal off the conservatory, so that the remainder of the restaurant was usable.

I was cashing up after Sunday lunch time opening when there was a knock on the door. All the staff had left, except for Ben who was in the kitchen with a radio blaring while he tidied up.

Thinking that may be somebody had left a coat or some other item behind, I went to answer it. As I opened the door, it was given a hard shove causing me to stumble backwards and wind up on my backside.

A bloke in motor cycle leathers and a race helmet was waving a sawn off twelve bore in my direction. "Get to the till and take all the notes out, and be bloody quick about it."

"Or what?" I retorted.

"This," he replied aiming a swift kick to my ribs.

The sharp pain made me wince. Not wishing to aggravate old injuries, I began to raise myself from the floor. Holding my side I made my way behind the bar and over to the till. As I made an attempt to shout to Ben for help, my assailant pushed the barrels of the shotgun against my mouth and told me to shut it. Not wishing to rile him further, I complied.

I reached for the notes in the drawer and placed then in a cloth coin bag.

"Now let's go the safe and get last nights takings."

"Last nights takings are in the nightsafe down at Lloyds, so unless you intend to raid the bank, you're out of luck."

"You're lying. They're here somewhere, I know it."

"Look in the back; you'll see another nightsafe wallet ready for today's takings. I walk to the bank every evening and deposit the wallet."

He grabbed the coin bag then brought the butt of the gun round in an arc and caught me on my chin. I began to sink to the floor as he made for the door. Grasping the edge of the counter I slowly sank to my knees, before passing out.

I could have only been unconscious for a matter of minutes but I was still groggy and dizzy as I tried to stand and reach for the phone. Scrolling through its memory I found Wendy's number. She answered almost immediately and I explained that my shotgun friend had returned. She explained she was on a rest day and I apologised and told her I would ring the station.

She insisted that she would do it and would be with me in twenty minutes. Having gained a little more of my senses I staggered to the kitchen to alert Ben. He grabbed me before I hit the floor again, and began to tend to the cuts on my face.

An ARV (armed response vehicle) arrived within five minutes of putting the phone down. I explained that the robber had already fled the scene, and no, I did not know in which direction.

Wendy turned up alongside an ambulance. She asked after my well-being and I realised that I was speaking oddly due to the blow to my jaw. The paramedics checked it out then told me I would have to have an x-ray. They did not think it was broken but there could be fracture. I would also require a couple of stitches. A scene of crimes officer would be along shortly and Wendy told me she would stay until I returned from the hospital.

Despite medical advice, to the contrary I declined an overnight stay. The jaw was not broken but had suffered considerable bruising which I could testify to, my ribs likewise were not broken but severely bruised, which again I could testify as correct. Rather than stitches, a couple of small narrow strips of sticky plaster were used to bring the cut together. I was told it lead to a less noticeable scar. I returned to The Old Bell.

Wendy had plenty of questions for me but my answers were scant., and talking was painful.

"Sorry Wendy but when he forced the door open, I fell back and landed with a hell of a bump on my arse. Then things happened so quick, I can hardly believe it myself. He told me to open the till and give him the cash and when at first I refused, he gave me a kick. He then asked for Saturdays takings but I told him they were banked in the nightsafe, which he believed. They're actually by my bed."

"Okay, but what do you remember about him? You're an ex job you know the drill."

"Yeah, yeah, I know. Well I'm five eleven and he was an inch or so taller than me. I couldn't see any facial details except he was white with brown eyes. His accent although distorted by his helmet sounded local. Oh, and his leathers were Belstaff, with no distinguishing marks. And that is about it."

"It's a lot more than I had ten minutes ago! And you reckon you were a copper!" Wendy laughed.

"With what I've given you and from what you learnt from the first attack, I'd say you still have bugger all. Does that sound about right to you?"

Wendy agreed and we chatted a while longer, drinking some fresh coffee, that Ben produced. There was also sandwiches, but it was too difficult for me to bite and chew. We decided that, as I appeared to be someone's target, that I should install a security camera. Discreetly, if possible.

Under the pretence of installing floodlights to cover the car park area, which would seem a prudent move, two cameras were also installed, disguised as part of the lighting system. A dummy camera was also installed, in full view, above the door.

One of the regulars to eat in the restaurant was my old Ghurkha friend, Ken. When he heard of the problems that I had encountered he wanted to ask serving friends of his to keep an eye on the pub. I explained that it was not practical as there may not be any further attacks, and even if there were, I would not be informed in advance.

More than three months elapsed and I became more relaxed about the situation, as the pain and bruising disappeared. Jane was still anxious over the matter, and often after closing I noticed she became nervous at any sudden noise.

It was a Tuesday evening. I had gotten rid of the last customer and Jane and I were washing the last of the glasses and emptying ash trays, Being a Tuesday, the restaurant took last orders at nine o'clock and Ben and his staff had already departed. In an amazingly quick movement, a leather clad assailant in full race helmet burst in to the bar area from behind the cellar door, brandishing his sawn off shotgun. Jane screamed and he grabbed her, placing his right arm around her neck and then pushing the barrels of the gun against her nostrils and yelling at her to shut up and for me to remain still.

I could see the horror in Jane's eyes and could feel the fear that was invading my own mind. My concern was not for me but for Jane.

I could see Jane was close to a full blown panic attack and thankfully she passed out and was allowed to fall, cracking her head on the floor.

The intruder turned his attention on me. "You know the drill, put the takings in a bag, and those from last night."

"Last nights are already banked. You're too late." I replied as calmly as I could.

"Don't bullshit me. I watched this place all last night and today and you ain't left the pub at all. So get it and quick." With that, he shoved the barrels in to my stomach.

"They're upstairs. I'll go get them."

"Hold it there and step away to the end of the bar. I'll just make sure the lady here doesn't try to be the hero." He produced some plastic cable ties and secured them around her ankles and wrists then balled up the cloth on the sink and placed it in Jane's mouth. Taking a glass drying cloth he wrapped it over her mouth and secured it behind her neck.

Taking a couple of steps towards me, he thrust the barrels in to my mid riff and told me to get up the stairs. All manner of scenarios went through my mind as to how I could foil him, but common sense told me to put any thoughts of heroism aside and just do as he asked. We climbed the staircase; I with the barrels pushed firmly in my back, and made our way to the bedroom.

"Get the cash and put it in the bag," he ordered throwing the coin bag in on the bed.

"You know you ought to think about getting out of the pub trade. It's a bloody dangerous occupation, especially for you." He laughed raucously at his attempt at humour. "Can't be a lot of profit in it either." He laughed again.

I bent down and reached under the bed, pulling out another cloth bag. As I placed it on the bed, he swung the shotgun and struck me on my right hand side ribcage. I groaned and fell face down on the bed only to sense the gun being raised again and then feeling it smash into my back.

On top of old injuries, the pain was agonising. I turned over and drew my knees and legs up under my chin. More blows reined in on to my side.

I tried to roll away and the last thing I remember was seeing the wooden stock descending towards my head.

CHAPTER 27

I had no idea where I was, but I did recognise the face peering at me. I was in bed and tried to roll towards Wendy, but the agonising pain caused by that effort defeated me. I silently screamed at the suffering it caused.

"Don't try and move Chas, I'll get a nurse now you're awake." Her shadow passed over me as she rose and made her way to the door.

"Wait," I croaked, "where am I? What happened? Get me some water, my throats parched."

Wendy turned back and placed a hand on my arm. "Okay, but for the moment keep quiet and I'll call the nurse." She reached above the bed and fiddled with something that I could not see.

A few moments later a nurse came in to the room. "So you're awake Mister Barker. How do you feel? Do you have any pain?"

"I don't know where the pain starts or where it finishes. Every part of me is suffering. What happened to me?"

The nurse took my wrist and checked my pulse, and then while checking my blood pressure she said, "You were brought in here having been badly beaten. For two days you have been drifting in and out of consciousness."

"Two days! What is today?" I could not comprehend what I was being told.

A tall man with grey hair entered the room and approached the bed. "Good afternoon mister Barker and how are we feeling? Any pain?"

"Yes." I replied thinking this must a standard, fits all scenario questions. "Considerable pain, is there anything you can do for me?"

He took the chart from the end of my bed then spoke to the nurse. "I will tell the nurse to give you a painkilling injection which can be repeated if necessary.. It should also help you sleep. Your body needs plenty of rest mister Barker. You have not suffered any lasting damage, but it will be a while before your back on an even keel. I'll pop in and see you again tomorrow. Try to get some rest."

I looked at Wendy. "Well that told me nothing. What happened that I've wound up in here feeling as though a train has hit me, and if I've been here two days, who the hell is looking after the pub?"

Wendy explained what had occurred. Jane could hear the intruder shouting and swearing at me. This was accompanied by thuds that she imagined were blows being delivered to my body. After a few minutes, the assailant came down the stairs and casually walked out the door. She heard him leave on a motor cycle, and dialled nine, nine, nine. She still has a sore head, but insists that you would want the pub opened as usual.

Try as I might I could not remember very much at all.

"Don't worry, the doc says that you'll either recall more later, or your brain will blot it out entirely." Wendy took a couple of grapes from the bunch on the side. "Jane has been absolutely wonderful. After everything that she went through, she insisted on returning to work and making sure the pub was open for business. You'll owe her big time when you get back. Although we don't have facial shots of matey boy, we do have a licence plate number and the make of the bike he was riding. Good idea the dummy camera and those disguised in the flood lamps." She took a few more grapes and in between mouthfuls told me that the bike was registered to a lad in Horsham but he had sold it six months ago. He also had alibis for the times of the attacks. The bike was paid for by cheque and the details have been requested. You know what banks are like . . . !"

Trying to smile was painful. "Still that's more than we had a week ago. I'd love to find out who the bastard is, preferably a day before you do."

Wendy put her hand on my arm. "Leave it Chas. We'll get the scrote, I promise you. Anyway, I don't think you'll be fit enough to dish out a hiding. You've gone soft since you retired."

I grimaced. "When I retired, I thought that my days of getting involved in fights and tussles with villains was over, especially following being shot. I'm beginning to think I was safer in than out."

I spent another six days in hospital. When I left for home, I could still feel every ache and pain. It brought back memories of my last stay in hospital. I just hoped the convalescence would not be so long.

Jane was overjoyed that I had returned, and was not at all crestfallen that I was about as much use as tits on a bull. I promised that I would do as much as I was able but she said not to overdo it as all the staff had done extra hours to cover and even Bert and Alice had popped over to see if any help was required. My mother had telephoned to ask when I was next coming over and Jane had told her that I had tripped and fallen and would phone her in a few days.

Wendy called to bring me up to date. "I called the hospital but they told me you had been discharged. Are you sure you were ready for that?"

"I was, and I think they were not too displeased to see the back of me. I've had enough of hospitals to last me a lifetime. I'm still as sore as hell but I'd rather be sore here, than there. I hope your ringing with some good news."

"The bank came up trumps and the owner lives in Newbury. Has a flat, but there is no sign of him at the moment. He was one of those arrested for affray when Club OMG was targeted. We can't tie him to Billy Maggs or Arthur Lee. He got off light at trial pleading he got caught up in events and was there with his girlfriend to enjoy a night out. Neighbours say he disappeared a few days ago. Name Troy Maynard mean anything to you? Got a string of minor offences, shoplifting, burglary, d and d and a more serious offence of GBH. Serving a suspended of two years at the moment. He'll show sooner or later."

"Name doesn't mean anything to me. Does he have any known associates that I might recognise?"

"No, he seems to work on his own. Drinks in his local, The Snooty Fox and the landlord and locals say although he gets on well with everybody he always appears to be a bit of a loner. As you will well know, because of the firearm involvement, every effort is being made to apprehend him. Pubs local to here and Newbury have been made aware and his picture has been circulated. We're trying to trace family and see if he's holed up with them or if they know of his whereabouts."

"Well let's pray that it won't be too long before the little bastard is behind bars. I won't keep you any longer but I'd be grateful for an update when you've got something." We said our goodbyes and I rang off.

CHAPTER 28

"Troy, just stay where you are. I don't care what you think, your mum told your uncle to sort this out, and he said you weren't to show your face outside of here, and as I don't want to cross him or even worse your mother, you damn well stay put. I don't know what you've done and I don't care but you ain't putting foot outside of that door." The person speaking to Troy was a man of swarthy complexion. Stockily built he was quite short at five feet eight inches and Troy knew better than to go up against him.

"He didn't mean that literally. He wouldn't want me to spend every minute of every day stuck here with you, and my mum didn't mean for me to be locked up. This is a fucking one bed council flat and your cooking skills are just about up to serving a glass of cold water Ted. My back aches from sleeping on that bloody camp bed and you play crap music all day long. I need to go out, get some fresh air and a decent pint and get my mum to cook me a decent meal."

"I've got beer in the fridge, we can order take away and we can even share my bed, it is a double, but there is no way your going through that door." Ted gave him a look that dared him to attempt it.

"I'm not sharing a bed with you. I'm not a fucking queer; I'd rather sleep on the floor."

"Your choice and I'm no shirtlifter either. I prefer to have the bed to myself anyway. Now decide, you can either have scrambled egg with me, or phone and order yourself something else."

Troy leaned back in an old armchair that had seen better days. Ted's flat left a lot to be desired. The carpet was filthy and had not been vacuumed for more than two months, ever since Ted's hoover packed up. The place smelt stale and had become progressively worse, with both of them living there. At least Ted put the rubbish out in the bin every night.

Troy understood why he needed to keep his head down. He was lucky that the warning put out to the local publicans had alerted his uncle to the situation. He knew his uncle was only doing what his mother told him too. She ruled her little empire with a rod of iron and she would not blanch at dishing out a beating to him or any other member of the family if they crossed her. If she knew his uncle was involved in his dilemma she would have his nuts on a skewer. He still could not fathom out how the police had identified him. He was always careful to keep his helmet on and the motor bike was not registered in his name. On his last raid he had avoided the security camera over the door, and sneaked in round the back, after seeing the kitchen staff leave.

He acted on his own so there was nobody other than family to squeal on him. No, he must have been careless at sometime. He also knew he had to get out even for only an hour or so. He also knew he needed the company of a woman.

Meanwhile he would bide his time. Ted would go out tomorrow for beers and groceries. That would be his chance for a couple of hours of freedom and fuck what Ted, his mum, uncle or anyone else said. He lay back in the chair and closed his eyes.

※

I had been back at the pub for ten days now and although my ribs still hurt, I felt a lot better in myself. I had telephoned my mother and told her I was sorry it had taken so long to return her call, but I had been feeling unwell. Strange but she said she had not called me and I had visited her only two or three days ago. I made up my mind to visit her.

Jane was making an admirable job of running the pub, and was quite happy to continue when I asked if she could do another two or three days. Chatting to her, over a coffee, I discovered that a few years ago she had lived with her partner here in Yateley but the relationship foundered and he moved away leaving her with a house and mortgage. She struggled for a while but found herself a couple of lodgers paying their rent in cash. With the bar work she managed to keep her head above water. There had been a couple of short-lived affairs, but no mister right.

She thanked me for providing her with a steady job again. I in turn thanked her for the hours she had put in, especially while I was in hospital.

I told her I was off to visit my mother but would be back for the evening shift, for what help I was.

Taking it steady I drove to my mothers and found a carer there preparing some pre-packaged meal for her lunch. It was Leanne the one with the long blonde hair. She was quite taken aback with the discoloration that was still apparent on my face. She went through to the kitchen to prepare some food and a drink for my mother.

I sat with my mother who did not seem to notice the bruising on my face although it had faded considerably, or that I grimaced when I made to lift the chair next to where she was sat down. Leanne came in and put the food in front of my mother, and then looked at me, and with her eyes indicated I should follow her in to the kitchen.

"Is my mother okay?" I asked.

"Yes and no." She replied. "Her memory is a little worse but I was more concerned with a lump I found on her breast when I showered her this morning. I think you should get a doctor to examine her. By the way, what's happened to you? You look awful."

"Thanks, you've made me feel better already."

"Sorry, I meant your face is bruised and you seem stiff with every movement you make."

"Somebody robbed the pub and gave me a beating. Had a couple of days in hospital, which is why I haven't been around. Still, I'm getting over it. I'm more bothered by what you've just told me. I'll ring her quack in a moment. Meanwhile don't say anything to my mum about the robbery or my injuries. At the moment she hasn't noticed a thing, so we'll let it lie."

"Look, I'm no expert, and it may well be nothing. Your GP will probably refer you to the hospital for x-rays and tests. And don't worry I won't say a thing to your mum about the state you're in" She smiled and touched me lightly on the arm. "You ever thought of taking up a safer occupation?"

"No." I laughed. "Thanks for that, and you're right, regarding the lump. Let's wait until we know what it is."

Leanne cleared away the empty dishes, then left and I sat with my mother until she fell asleep.

Arriving back at the pub I explained to Jane what I had learnt. She immediately offered to accompany me to the hospital with my mother, if that was the outcome of the GP visit, which she told me was more than likely. She disclosed that she had experienced the same thing two years previously, but that she had been lucky and it proved to be a cyst.

The two of us opened and worked the bar that evening, but at nine o'clock I told her to have an early night. The restaurant was fairly quiet and last orders were taken at eight thirty and the staff were gone by ten fifteen. I went to bed that evening having made a mental note to be at my mothers the next morning when her GP had arranged to call.

Just as predicted, the doctor made a quick examination then told me that she would arrange for a hospital appointment. I asked that the hospital contact me on my mobile to make any arrangements.

CHAPTER 29

The following week, I, along with Jane, took my mother to the Royal Berkshire Hospital where she underwent x-rays and a biopsy. The consultant told me he would be writing to her GP but that the lump was small and it would appear to have been caught nice and early.

I took my mother home and waited until the carer arrived. I had been hoping it was Leanne so that I could thank her for the care she provided and for noticing the lump, but it was another woman who I had not before. Her name was Ann and she told me Leanne would be back the following day. Jane and I said our goodbyes and left for Yateley.

The lunchtime trade was over when I returned to The Old Bell. Bert and Alice, who had insisted on helping out, were just finishing tidying around. When I remarked that the part-time staff could cover, they reminded that when Bert was ill I had helped them with no pay, and they were glad to reciprocate, and if further visits and treatment were necessary they would be there to help again.

Overall, I thought that the kindness shown by Jane, Bert, Alice and Leanne was astounding. People I had known for only for a short while, but between them they had provided a friendship I found hard to comprehend.

I was still mulling this over in my mind when the ringing of the telephone returned me to the present. It was Wendy.

"Good news Chas. Our friend Troy is in custody. He's not saying much, but I think when he learns the seriousness of his crime, he will cough. I'll let you know."

"Thanks Wendy. How did you manage to catch up with him?"

"Public spirited young bar lady. Young Troy was getting frustrated and rang an agency for company. The girl they sent round not only does escort business but also works in bars. She recognised him from the picture circulated to the licensed trade and after concluding her business with him rang the station and told us where he was staying. I told her she could have been in danger but she wanted her eighty quid and wasn't going to pass it up! When I told her the breweries and LVA had offered a one thousand pound reward, that she was in line to collect, she couldn't believe it."

"There's more to this than just the robberies. You need to find out who is behind it all. Somebody was targeting me, and I'd like to know who."

The following day Wendy rang again to tell me Troy Maynard had been remanded in custody, and she was investigating his background. At the moment, Maynard was still unwilling to talk and would not even give a reason for the attacks. In particular, she was probing family and links to known criminals, especially Billy Maggs or Arthur Lee, who would have cause to hold a grievance against me.

It was a few days before I heard from Wendy again.

"He thinks he's such a clever little sod. Says nothing but 'no comment' and believes we will not learn anything. A search of his flat turned up a passport, with the next of kin in case of accident etcetera completed, with the contact given as a Sally Edwards. Further investigation shows she was formerly Sally Prictoe and was the mother of a child Troy Prictoe. He later took what we believe is his fathers name and she married a Clive Edwards, who if you remember your early days in the force, was a lending shark and brothel owner. Sally Edwards has convictions for soliciting, but nothing else. He disappeared years ago and has never been seen since. Rumour is that she had him taken care of. She is a nasty piece of work, still selling girls through an escort agency, but is also involved in the property market, drugs, and money lending. It explains why Troy is keeping his mouth shut. She'd probably cut his tongue out if he implicated her. Lot of her business is conducted through an offshore company which means we will never find much out about her business associates."

"Sounds like a lovely lady, but I've never heard of her. Not under any of those names, although I do recall Clive Edwards. He was a particularly nasty piece of work. My money is still on Maggs and Lee, but that's only because I can't think of anybody else with a grudge. Thanks for phoning and let me know how you get on. Speak soon."

"Will do Chas, and look after yourself." She laughed and then added, "At least better than you have done so far.," and rang off.

After speaking with Wendy, I began to wrack my brain over the names Prictoe, Edwards and Maynard. Not one of them rang a bell. I was completely immersed in my own thoughts, when Jane entered the room.

"Sorry if I made you jump Chas, but I was wondering if you're available to discuss the new menu. You know how uppity Ben gets every time we change the menu; well at least, he proposes changing it and you turn it down."

"I have looked at it and because he's left the most popular dishes on there, even though he says it's only run of the mill pub grub, I'm willing to let him have his way with one proviso. I want cheese and biscuits back on the desert menu and I'd like something different or at least a bit out of the ordinary. Also tell him I hope he's costed and priced this up correctly, I don't want to see margins falling. Say Chas says if it runs at a loss I'll take it from his salary."

She smiled and said, "You can tell him that last bit yourself. He scares me when he has a knife in his hand."

"You're scared of him, but I thought you two had become an item. A couple of the locals told me they had seen you out together."

"Not so much an item, but we do enjoy each others company. Ben's good fun outside of that kitchen, just bloody scary inside it."

Hospital, the attacks, police interviews and filling in insurance claims meant that more and more of the day-to-day running of the pub was falling on Jane and

Ben's shoulders. I made a mental note to have a chat with each of them, and let them know it had not gone unnoticed. Despite all that had happened takings were rising and profits were good.

CHAPTER 30

A week went by with me hearing nothing from Wendy. I knew what it was like when I was on the force with people telephoning for progress, when there was not any to tell, so I refrained from making the call, but found the wait frustrating.

To occupy my mind I concentrated on the business. Every part of it appeared to be running smoothly and profitably. This made it harder to put Maynard to the back of my mind. If someone had a grudge against me, why could I not fathom out who it was. I had put away a few criminals in my time but other than Maggs. Lee and Oldfield, none of them were for really serious crime. Most career criminals expected to get caught and serve time at some point in their chosen occupation, and accepted the consequences of their actions. Who ever it was would be in need of police protection, if I got to them first.

My thoughts had strayed again and I forced myself to deliberate on the direction I wanted my life and business to take. Additionally there was my mother to consider. Would I be happy if she was placed in a home?

Although the decision had been mine, I had entered the licensed trade almost by accident. Martin and I still spoke occasionally and now his mental state was that much better he enjoyed passing on his knowledge, and answering my questions. Each time we chatted, he would be extremely regretful for suddenly leaving me in the lurch, and as much as I told him the apology was not necessary, he still went through this same ritual.

Even after the capital outlay for the purchase and renovation of The Old Bell, I still had money in the bank, a substantial house in Wokingham, free of mortgage, a police pension and income from the pub. My expenses were minimal, I ate at the pub most days, I rarely went out and if I did it was nowhere expensive, and I had not had a holiday. My love life was almost non-existent, except for the odd short affair with old acquaintances. My life and business barring the last little problem was ticking over very nicely, thank you.

Last problem! That is what really irked me. For twenty-four years, I was a copper and fifteen of those were spent in CID. I was a detective and could not even work out who was trying to damage or ruin either me, or my business, or both. Detective sergeant that was my rank and the chances are I would have retired the same unless luck had intervened. I had no wish to be an Inspector.

Maybe now was not the time to mull over the path I wished my life to take. Too much going on and if I was brutally honest with myself, I had no idea.

My cogitation was disturbed by Jane entering the room and pulling up a chair to sit beside me.

"Are you alright Chas? Only you seem to be in a world of your own."

I smiles at her. "I'm okay Jane, I was just thinking of life in general. I never set out to be a pub landlord, mind you, I never set out to be a copper either. I wanted to be a teacher, math and history, those were my subjects, and I actually had a place at Bulmershe Teacher Training College. Sometimes I wish I'd gone ahead with it. I was a lot more idealistic in those days, but instead, the idea of money in my pocket at the end of each month won out and I joined the police. You worrying about me are you. No need, I'm still the same miserable old fart I was before that bang on the head."

She laughed. "That's one thing your not. You're a lovely guy and definitely did not deserve that beating. Do you want a cup of tea, I'm just about to make one before I have to open?"

"I'd love one, please Jane. Sorry I left you on your own. I hadn't noticed how the time had got on. How's your love life? Still with that scary chef?"

Jane gave me a knowing smile then went through to the kitchen to make a pot of tea. I returned to my deliberations, without I must add little success.

The next day my old governor, John Chivers telephoned and gave me some surprising news. First he wanted to know how well I knew Andrew Strong and Owen Strong. Replying in the affirmative I gave him a brief history of our past. The revelation was Troy Maynard was their nephew through their half sister Sally Edwards. This was discovered when researching her dealings and linking her through MYOB Holdings that held a substantial stake in the Pub and Club company Limited.

Although it could not be proved, it was suspected that when the picture of Maynard was circulated around the pubs that one of the uncles immediately recognised Troy and found him somewhere to stay. Both they and Maynard strenuously denied that. Maynard had been found staying with a known associate of both the Strong brothers and Sally Edwards, called Ted Szewcyk. Not a person I had come across before. A low life with a string of minor offences.

Harking back to my disputes with the brothers, in particular, Andy, I ventured that he put Troy up to causing the mayhem. John agreed that it was likely, but Troy insisted no one else was involved, and unless evidence to the contrary was found, then Troy would take the rap for the crimes. Maynard had been charged with robbery with violence, assault occasioning actual bodily harm and various other offences. He was to remain in custody until trial.

The months went by and the takings continued to rise, especially for the restaurant. On a trip to north London Jane and Ben were strolling round a market and tasted a chutney made from pomegranate and kiwi with a little heat, added by the addition of chillies.

Ben was quite taken with the taste and walked over to a cheese stall, purchased some cheddar, returned to the chutney stall and tasted the two together.

Exclaiming that the taste was exquisite, he introduced himself to the owner, a woman called Rebecca. Her business was called *Beccas Pepper Pots* and she was known as Becca. Ben explained that he required a supply of the chutney in small pots big enough for an individual serving with some leftover. He also wanted the label to read, *specially prepared for The Old Bell by Beccas Pepper Pots*. He agreed that Becca could add her website, telephone number, whatever for advertising purposes.

Initially he wanted fifty jars to see if his idea would work and if successful he could see this increasing to two or three hundred a month Becca produced a variety of different sized pots and one was decided upon. Delivery would be a week.

When Ben showed me the pot he had brought back from his trip, and I tasted the goods. I pronounced it was delicious, but why did he not order a catering size jar and serve it in the small dishes we already had. Ben just stared at me, called me a philistine and told me it was in the presentation as people ate with their eyes! I left him to it.

A week later, when the goods arrived I watched carefully to see how Ben was serving his new found chutney. It was served with the cheese board, ploughman's lunch, and most cold meat dishes. I considered the portions too large until I noticed that when the servers collected the empty plates they popped the half empty chutney jars in to a small bag for the customer to take away. Over eighty per cent of customers were delighted to take their half-eaten chutney home and some even enquired if they could purchase one or two jars for friends. The pub now had a sideline of selling various chutneys through the restaurant.

CHAPTER 31

The months went by and finally, Maynard was found guilty, and sentenced to eighteen years. Troy had remained loyal to his family, and denied any involvement of others. Andy, his brother Owen and a woman I took to be Sally Edwards all scowled at me at the court and Andy came over threatening to deal with me later. His sister grabbed him and pulled him back making some remark that Troy would not be in this predicament if it were not for him. Enlightening I thought.

With that episode of my life now over, I returned to giving consideration to my future. I was undecided about the pub trade. The finding, purchasing and renovation of The Old Bell had been satisfying and as much as I enjoyed the bar work, I preferred to stand back and play mine host whilst the staff served the customers. Never the less, I would not mind finding another pub to work my magic on.

Earlier in the month, my accountant had telephoned to discuss my tax liability. He remarked that most businesses in their first year or two showed a loss and were able to mitigate any tax liability. I on the other hand even with improvements to the premises was going to show a profit, due mainly to having a low creditor position as I had not borrowed for the purchase and therefore had no heavy interest charges to offset my profit. My own simple mind still reckoned a profit was preferable to paying some bank interest and charges, just to obviate any tax due.

※

"That's twice that bastard has caused this family grief. We ought to nail his arse to the wall once and for all." Andy's face was contorted with rage. "First he does for me and then he gets our Troy banged up."

"For Christ's sake Andy, just shut up. The reason Troy is inside is because he listened to you two tossers. He was a fucking copper for Christ's sake did you not think he might be bright enough to outwit you two dimwits. Now listen to me and listen good. You do not go near Barker or his pub or anything else of his. You do not mention his name and you do not encourage anybody else to do your bidding, have you got that straight. Troy may be as stupid as you two, but he is still my son, and I am pissed off that he is serving time because of you and you." Sally looked at each brother in turn. Even in her high heels she was only five feet six inches, and she gave rise to the saying, a face like a bag of nails. She was of slight build and dressed in a pin stripe business suit. The face was overdone with black eye make up and pink lipstick.

"But he owes us Sal. You can't just let him get away with it."

"I can and I will. He owes me nothing and if it wasn't for you numbnuts," she poked her finger in Andy's chest, "I wouldn't be involved. There is far too much at stake to be sidetracked by you two's need to get even. I can't afford to have the old bill poking their noses in to my business, and don't forget the only reason you two have a couple of pubs and clubs, is because I provide the money."

"Those pubs and clubs provide you with a lot of money. Your dealers know they can operate in them without fear of being grassed to the coppers. And the tills provide you with the means to launder the drug money."

Sally looked at the two brothers. ".Don't ever let me hear you mention my business outside of these four walls. You in particular Andy need to learn to button your lip. I'm off and don't forget what I've just told you. Stay clear of Barker. If I hear anything I shan't be looking for him, I shall be looking for you." She walked out, slamming the door behind her.

Andy looked at Owen. "I don't care what she says, that shit Barker has crossed me at every turn and I aim to make the bastard pay. Sally might be the one with the money but she doesn't fucking own me."

"Maybe she doesn't but if you go against her orders she'll cut you off without a penny, and not only cut off the pennies, but your balls as well." Owen laughed as he made the last remark.

"Have I got enough money to buy another pub, that's all I'm asking Joe." Chas was sat across from Joe Harrison, a senior partner at Henshall Whyte, the same accountants that Martin had used. They knew the licensed trade inside out and had many contacts within the pub trade which was very useful to a newcomer like me. I thought back to when I initially joined Martin, and on meeting Barry and Amy for the first time, told them that I was considering entering the pub trade. I fibbed that Martin was an old friend and had given me carte blanche to study his business set up. Now here I was trying to emulate Martin's set up.

"Chas, as I've tried to explain, you have enough funds without borrowing to buy a small concern that maybe facing hard times or a bigger place with potential that needs renovating and a bit of TLC. The first is a risk and for the second you will not have the monies to pay for the necessary work." Joe leaned back in his chair and took a mouthful of coffee, looking at me for some sort of response.

I did not really have one. I knew he was telling me the truth. "I don't know Joe. What about my house?"

"We agreed a long time ago that house was always to be kept separate from the business. Just supposing the whole lot goes tits up and you lose every penny. At least you'll still have your house and a police pension so there will always be a roof over your head and enough income to pay the bills. My advice is still, leave the house out of it."

"Okay. When I have my sensible head on, I know you're right. What you're telling me is that for what I want to do I need another hundred grand or so. That about right?"

"In a nutshell yes. But you still have to find the right place even if you have the money in place."

I drained the last of the coffee from my cup. "Thanks Joe. I'll go away and think about it. And by the way that coffee is bloody awful, either you need to teach your secretary to make coffee or buy a machine that will do it for her." I got up and went to the door then turning back as Joe was rising to from his chair to see me out, said, "You and Ginny, that's your secretary's name isn't it, both of you come over the pub next week and enjoy my hospitality for a change. Sit down Joe, I'll see myself out, all this rising and sitting down again, it's like a bloody lodge meeting. See you next week, don't forget."

CHAPTER 32

Jane, Ben and myself sat in my private kitchen upstairs drinking tea and eating biscuits.

"So tell me do you think it appeals to you in anyway? Be honest because it's a big commitment you'd be making." I had pondered over the problem of raising capital and a couple of days ago whilst working the bar I realised that I could solve two problems at once. Offer Jane and Ben the opportunity to purchase forty per cent of The Old Bell and take over the management of it taking a salary and a share of the profits each year. That way the two most valuable staff members would be in control and residence and I would have the funds for my next project.

Ben spoke. "What you say is really appealing and I like the idea of taking responsibility for the running of the pub. Provided of course all that you have told us is fact. What safeguards would there be?"

"Just as I told you Ben, but before we go any further, what do you think Jane?"

"I'm still trying to get my head round it. I've always dreamt of having my own pub, but always thought it would be as a manager for someone else. How easy would it be to get the money to pay for it?"

"I don't have all the answers, but Joe Harrison who you both know, will help sort the mechanics of it out for all of us. As I said the place is worth four hundred K which means forty per cent is one sixty K. Because of all that has happened and your contribution to the business over the past year then I am willing to allow you to purchase your share for one hundred and thirty thousand. I will want to see month end figures and if everything looks kosher, then I will not interfere with day to day running. I can't be fairer than that. Look, if I didn't think the pair of you were up to it, then I wouldn't make the offer. There will be safeguards in place, such as if any of us should die, or wish to sell, but if you agree to proceed in principle, then I'm sure between us we can sort out any problems."

I watched as they looked at each other then turning towards me nodded, and in unison spoke their concurrence. I told them I would arrange for all of us to get together with Joe, but in order to protect themselves they should find their own solicitor, either for the pair of them, or individually.

It was decided to establish a limited company for the business and it took almost six months to finalise arrangements and for me to receive the funds. My search for another pub now began in earnest.

I spent hours travelling to view various establishments, but finding one that suited my requirements was more difficult than I had envisaged. I had registered with every commercial agent dealing in licensed premises I could find, but to no avail. All I desired was a pub with scope to develop a restaurant business and increase bar capacity.

After more than three months of looking, I found an olde worlde pub on the outskirts of Thatcham. With an asking price of only one hundred and twenty five thousand, it was a snip. Freehold with large garden and car park, the original part of the building was circa sixteen hundred and eighty five. Thatcham was one of England's earliest known villages and was famous for the reed beds that abounded and accounted for the popularity of thatched properties in the area.

There were two bars plus usual amenities downstairs and upstairs were a kitchen, bathroom living room and two bedrooms. There was an old below ground cellar, that also doubled as a storeroom. Turnover was only just over twenty five thousand per annum with gross profit of fifty eight per cent. This was on beer sales plus the usual crisps, nuts and pork pies. There was no kitchen for the bar and the present owners admitted they did not feel able to spend their saved capital on this item at this time of their lives. Eight years ago, they had looked at putting a restaurant, for thirty to forty covers, and kitchen on the rear, but had not gone ahead. The original plans were available although would need resubmitting.

I told them I was very interested and offered one hundred and twenty thousand plus stock at valuation. They took my number and said they would telephone me in two days with their response, as there was another party interested in the property. I was not sure that was the truth, but I was happy to give them a day or so to consider my offer.

Two days later, I heard from the agents, Brown and Company, and was disheartened to be told that another buyer had offered the asking price. Bearing in mind the potential for the business, I increased my offer to one hundred and twenty seven and a half thousand. The following day Browns telephoned again to pass on the information that the price had increased to one hundred and thirty thousand. Not wishing to get in a bidding war, I dropped out of the race. Time to look again.

Another month passed and I had not seen a single pub that tempted me in to even making a silly offer. Driving back to Wokingham after another wasted viewing I stopped at a small village pub for a shandy and some lunch.

Getting in to conversation with the landlord whose name I learnt was Vic, he told me for two hundred and fifty thousand I could have his pub as long as I took the wife that would be thrown in for free. I declined.

"If you want a nice little pub with potential there's one in Mortimer belonging to, bugger can't remember his name but I know it's going on the market in the next month or so." He turned his head towards the door through to the back. "Jeanie, what's the name of the bloke that has The Victory that wants to sell?"

An attractive slim woman of medium height came through the door. "Henry. Henry Sims, thinks he's Gods gift to women. Makes my skin crawl. No wonder his wife left him." She pulled a face to show her distaste.

Vic looked at her and said, "This is his brother, he popped in to find out how to get to Mortimer."

Jeanie's face dropped, and then as the penny dropped she slapped Vic on his arm. "You lying sod, if he was his brother he'd know his bleeding name."

Vic laughed. "Yeah but you should have seen the look on your face. It was a picture. Do you know if he's still wanting to sell?"

"He's bloody well got to. His ex wants her share and he can't raise the readies to pay her off. He's only been there three years or so and he's ruined the place. Could be a nice little pub that one, there's nobody else within a couple miles of him." She turned towards me. "You thinking of buying then? Let me know and I'll tell his wife, Carol, well ex wife, she can't wait for it to be gone, and him with it."

"Might be, if the price is right and the potential is there. However, Vic has offered me this place with you thrown in. I'm considering his offer."

She looked back over her shoulder as she returned through to back. "You'd never last the pace!"

Vic looked at me. "Now you know why the price is so cheap!"

I told him I was off over to Hermitage tomorrow to have a look at a likely purchase that Browns had told me was new on the market. I told Vic I would drive back through Mortimer, and take a look at The Victory.

Interesting was how I would describe my trip to Hermitage. The vendor said pubs in the area were fetching a good price. One just down the road in Thatcham made over the asking price. When I asked if he knew who had brought the place he told me it was a couple of brothers. There name was Strong and they were not particularly liked in the trade.

Barrel of Lies

Calling in at The Victory on my way home, I met Henry, the landlord. He was about five feet eight inches and at least two stone overweight. Wearing round gold framed spectacles, he reminded me of the Billy Bunter character as portrayed by Gerald Campion. The bar was empty, except for an old man and woman supping on two half pints.

Keeping my voice low I asked him if the rumour was true that he wished to sell.

"I could be." He looked away. "But I've not made my mind up yet. I've no real need to sell, but I have this hankering to open a bar in Phuket, where I've spent a few holidays and have grown to like the area. It's a big move to make and I've not yet decided which way to go."

Playing him at his own game I replied, "Oh well, if you decide you want to sell give me a call, my numbers on my card. Could save you a few thousand in agent's fees. I should tell you I am actively looking for a pub so if it's not in the near future I may already have found somewhere." I handed him my card with my mobile number on it. Drinking up I said my goodbye and left for home.

Deciding to call on my mother I noticed the carers car was parked in the drive. Entering the house I could hear singing and laughter. Entering the sitting room I could see Leanne and my mother singing old World War Two songs.

"Didn't think you'd know the words to those old tunes." I remarked.

"Your mums been teaching me over the past few months, haven't you Gwen?"

"And she's a fast learner." Butted in my mum.

I laughed. "I called to see if mum was alright but I can see she's as happy as a sand boy. Thanks, I know she looks forward to your calling and now I know why."

I stopped a while longer and told them all about my search for a pub. I did not mention that I had lost one to old enemies. Leanne left and I sat and watched Neighbours on the TV with my mother, sitting in the chair next to her. I dropped off to sleep.

I awoke with a start when I heard the front door open and somebody walk in. I was scrambling to get out of the chair when a voice called out, "Are you okay Gwen?" It was Leanne and I realised it was eight o'clock and Leanne was back to put mum to bed. I kissed my mother goodbye, and said cheerio to Leanne on my way out.

Wednesday morning I had to drive to Theale. There was an old pub on the outskirts of this large village area just to the south of Reading, that the agent told me the brewery were wishing to offload, as it was not in their plans for the future. I had some doubts as to whether it met my wishes but the price sounded good and it would not hurt to cast an eye over it.

I was surprised by the condition of the interior. It must have had a complete renovation within the last twelve months. The exterior was in need of tidying up, but nothing major. I asked the manager how he found things. He explained that he was put in three months ago when the previous manager left with a weeks takings and a barmaid. The week's takings were enhanced by the sale of all the bottled and dry stock and a couple of casks of lager! The police were still looking for him.

Business was slow and most locals used other pubs in the area. Still the potential was there, with scope for food. The asking price of only one hundred thousand sounded reasonable and I asked the agent to put in an offer of ninety thousand. From his response, I was quietly confident that it would be accepted.

The afternoon was to be all mine. I was giving the search for a pub a rest and in the evening I was going to show my face in The Old Bell and hopefully get a seat in the restaurant.

The restaurant was fully booked which was surprising for a Wednesday, but fortunately, a young couple that were regulars invited me to join them. Out of courtesy, I refused but they insisted and said it would be there way of saying thank you for giving them such a good deal for their wedding reception. I agreed, provided I picked up the drinks bill.

That was a mistake, we got through two and a half bottles of wine and a couple of brandy's. I had to have a taxi home, although Jane had said I could sleep there.

CHAPTER 33

The next morning I was having a quiet hour or two at home drinking black coffee and swallowing aspirin when my mobile rang. It was the business agent.

Trying to gather my faculties, and take in what he said, I thought "What do mean a higher offer has already been accepted." The agent explained that just on closing the following evening a new buyer had telephoned with an increased offer, that the brewery had accepted and had instructed him to take it off the market.

My brain was in no position to make much sense out of it, so I decided it was not to be. I had looked at six pubs over the last few weeks and all of those I had put an offer on had gone to a higher bidder, in some cases above asking price. I lay back in my armchair for a few minutes of restful sleep.

The chirping of the mobile disturbed my slumber. It was Henry from The Victory.

"Been thinking about what you said to me yesterday, you know selling the pub. What price are you willing to pay?"

"Hold on a minute Henry." I tried to gather my thoughts. "Yes I'm interested in buying the Victory but I think to satisfy both of us we should have a valuer look at it. If we can decide on a mutually acceptable valuer then I will meet the valuation."

From the sound Henry made the other end of the line I could see him thinking that a valuation may well come out fairly low. To help him come to a decision I added, "Whatever the valuation I will pay you an extra five thousand in cash which you will not need to declare to anybody."

"Couldn't make it ten could you?"

"No, but I will go to six, and that is my final offer. There is a condition though. You do not say a word about this to anyone until the deal is finalised, and I won't say a word either."

Although I had only spoken to him briefly, yesterday, I gleaned that the idea of cash on the side would help sway his mind. I would have probably gone to a maximum of twenty thousand in cash but I was not going to pay any more than I had to.

"Henry, this may seem strange but when you arrange for the valuation, I do not want my name mentioned. Tell them its in anticipation of selling, if the need should arise. If it is then any deal is off. Just as you wish to keep any cash deal quiet, so I need to remain anonymous, at least for the present. Can you do that?"

"Yeah. That's no problem, and I won't even ask why."

"Good. Tomorrow I'll give you a choice of agents to approach. Decide who you want to use and give them the instruction. I will pay the full valuation cost. If you don't like any of them, tell me who you want and I'll make a decision on whether we use them. Can you do that?"

"Yeah. Yeah leave it with me and I'll give you a bell." He rang off.

I was pretty sure that the Strong brothers were thwarting my every move to find a pub and so far they were in to purchasing two that I had been after. There funds could not be limitless so they would have to stop at some stage.

※

"What the fuck have you two arseholes been up to?" The voice that both Andy and Owen dreaded was ringing in their ears even from twenty feet away. The door that had been pushed open with force now slammed back to its shut position with a crash. Diminutive she may be but Sally Edwards entrance in to the busy bar was enough to make any man quake. She strode towards the bar where the brothers were standing. Patrons moved out of her way, silenced and staring, as she approached Andy and Owen.

Andy opened his mouth and started to speak.

"Shut it you stupid little man. I'll tell you when I want you to speak." She stepped closer to Andy who backed up half a step against the bar.

"Sal, lets go in to the back where you can tell us what the problem is. Come on I'll get . . . ."

"I told you to shut it, and no, we won't go in to the backroom. How about we let these nice people know what a pair of dumb pricks I have for brothers. Tell them how I am buying another two pubs I don't fucking want or need. Tell them how I have even paid a twelve thousand deposit on one of them and I didn't even know I had issued the cheque. Tell them how you are going to return my money."

Andy was getting redder and redder in the face and looked as if he would deliver a punch to Sally, notwithstanding that she was his sister, or at least half sister. "I can explain . . ." began Andy before Sally pushed a finger in to his chest and again told him to shut up, which he did.

Sally turned and looked at the customers who were fascinated by the scene being played out in front of them. "You lot can piss off." She turned back to the brothers. "Right you two in to the back room and this had better be good because if it's what I think it is you'll wish you'd never been born." The three moved away from the bar area as there were whistles and jeers from the crowd.

Andy and Owen took a seat but Sally remained standing. "Come on then, let's hear what you've got to say."

"They're investments to add to the existing portfolio. We've got them at a good price and there were other interested buyers. A few bob tarting them up and we'll be raking it in." Andy looked pleased with himself.

Sally glanced at Owen. "Don't you have anything to say?"

"No. I think Andy has said it all and to be honest I wasn't really involved." Owen had figured that Sally was not at all pleased and tried to distance himself from the purchase of the two pubs, which in itself was true, as

Andy had not sought his advice, only informed him of his buying spree.

"Just as I thought. The one with shit for brains doing his own thing just to get back at Chas Barker. I thought I made it fucking clear that you were to forget all about Barker, but no, you go spending my money on some pointless vendetta. Every problem you have with Barker is of your own making because you're so bloody stupid Andy. Well here's some news for you. I do not have the money to finance two new pubs and having spoken to my solicitor, I will likely lose the deposit you paid because I am not going ahead with the purchase. Actually, I am not going to lose it, I am taking it back from you Andy. From now on, you will draw just one thousand a month for wages, and you will not be replacing your car in two months. Not only did you try to buy those pubs, but you were willing to pay over the odds, with my money, just to stop Barker from getting them. You're finished as a partner in this business. You can have a job, but that's it. You will no longer sign cheques on behalf of the company and your position is assistant manager to Owen. Owen, I'm trusting you to put a stop to his shenanigans or he is out. You have control but you will not sign cheques over two thousand in value. I will countersign when necessary. He's your brother, sort him out."

Andy just stared at Sally and then spat out, "You're treating me like a fucking kid. You can't do that. I'll resign."

Before he could say any more Sally interrupted. "I'll accept 'cos the only reason your still here is because of mum. I was this close to just sacking you." She held her thumb and index finger about quarter of an inch apart. "Owen, keep him busy bottling up or something, 'cos that's all he fit for. I'm off, but I'm trusting you to control him."

After she had left, Andy looked at Owen and sneeringly mouthed. "No. *I think Andy has said it all and to be honest I wasn't really involved.*" Andy repeated Owen's words. "Fucking good brother you turned out to be."

"Hang on a minute Andy, I told you not to start making silly offers on pubs we didn't want or need. And as for paying a deposit, you have to have a screw loose."

"Well if you think you're going to be giving me orders then forget it."

"No Andy, it is as Sally said, you either begin to act sensibly or you will be gone, and with your track record I can't see you finding it easy to find a number as cushy as this. Bite the bullet, knuckle down and wait for this to blow over. You know what Sal's like. Give it a while and she'll take you back in the fold."

"Bite the bullet. Give it a while. What do you think I am, a fucking sheep. Take me back in the fold. You're a bigger arsehole than she is."

"Maybe but if you want to keep the job you've still got, you'd better remember, I'm your boss."

"Yeah well, that may not be for long. I've got plans. You wait and see, I'll have Barker and a business of my own." Andy stormed off cursing everything and everybody.

CHAPTER 34

The valuer was found, and a week later, he came back with a figure. Lower than Henry wished for and higher than I had imagined. I could live with stock at valuation and the price for a going concern with freehold but I would argue the point of five thousand pounds for the goodwill. What goodwill, Henry had run the pub in to the ground. Including the goodwill it was still a good price for what I had in mind.

I spent the next day disseminating the valuers report and finding nothing untoward arranged to meet Henry the following day.

Generally, the meeting went well but when I broached the question of goodwill, Henry was adamant it was a fair figure.

"Chas the figure is arrived at by a respected professional and is based on the last set of profit and loss accounts."

"Henry those figures are over twelve months old and your turnover is now a third of what it used to be. Take those nuts you sold me the other day. They were over a month outside their sell by date. Stock is remaining on the shelf because you no longer have the footfall through the bar to sell the quantity you still order."

"Ah, but the custom is latent it will return."

"Henry it's not hidden, it's in the pub down the road. Its bloody well lost!"

Henry shrugged his shoulders and reached behind to top up the whiskey in his glass. "We agreed that the price would be the valuation as supplied by the mutually acceptable valuer. Now I'm willing to stick to that and I hope you will to. If so then lets have a drink to celebrate."

"You're right Henry the agreement was the valuation figure and yes I will have a drink with you to celebrate. Don't forget the other part of the arrangement. You are not to go public with this sale until contracts are exchanged or its all off."

"Okay! Okay! But I still don't understand why the need for secrecy."

"And that remains a secret too Henry." I took the proffered whiskey and we raised our glasses in a toast.

Leaving The Victory I drove over to see Joe Harrison.

I sought his advice on how I could purchase The Victory and keep my ownership concealed. Not easy, he explained but not impossible. He asked for a couple of days to look in to it for me, and said he would give me a call when he had the answers.

My next move was to contact John and Sarah who I had met at The Falcon with Martin. I wanted two strong personalities when I reopened The Victory and these two had impressed me immensely on the first day that I met them. They say first impressions are the best, well if they would agree to join me, I would find out.

I drove to Lower Upwood to arrive just as the lunchtime was finishing. I had met them both a couple of times whilst working for Martin and we got on just fine. It was just gone two when I walked in to the bar.

"Chas, you old rogue, what brings you to this neck of the woods?"

"A cold drink and a proposition if you're interested. I'll have an OJ as I have to drive back and if there's a sandwich or roll hanging about I'll have that as well."

"Coming up. I'll get Sarah to get you something. She'll be pleased to see you."

I sat at the bar and reminisced with John, mostly about the times with Martin. By Half past two the last customer had left and John shut up shop. "I always close for the afternoon, there's not enough trade to stay open for. Now that the housing estate is finished, we get real busy in the evenings."

Sarah arrived with ham sandwiches and a bowl of chips. I asked her to stay, as I wanted a word with both of them.

"I'm buying another pub and I'd like to know if the two of you would be interested in managing it for me. I'll pay you more than you're getting now and a share of the profits. It won't be easy as the pub is in a rundown state and there will be some building work to contend with. Before I go any further, tell me are you interested?"

They looked at each other then Sarah said." Has somebody told you that we were thinking of leaving here?"

"No. Why are you jacking it in?"

"Don't get me wrong," John joined in, "But there were a couple of little problems with Pub and Club. One night I found some kid trying to push drugs in here. I had him straight out the door and told him if I saw him again I'd call the Old Bill. A few months later, I caught somebody else up to the same tricks. When I showed him the door, he said he had the owners permission. Well that got me and lifting him up by the scruff of his neck so as to bang his head on the beam over the porch, I pointed out that the name over the door was mine and I had not given any one permission to peddle drugs in my pub. For good measure I gave him a smack on the nose, which would have needed hospital treatment and told him if I saw him again he'd need an ambulance to get him home."

"Any more trouble since?"

"No but Andy Strong phoned to say the bloke was a friend of the family and they were not happy with the way I had treated him. I told him straight the next one to push drugs in my pub would be straight down the nick. We didn't part on very good terms and to be honest Chas, I can't work for someone like that."

"Well come and work for me then, you know I'm straight and everything will be above board. What do you say?"

Sarah smiled at me. "A month or two ago I'd have jumped at the chance, but we've been making plans to emigrate to Australia. I've got a brother out there with a building company, and he can give John work until we decide what we want to do."

I shrugged my shoulders. "Never mind. It would have been nice to have you with me on this one, but there you go."

John took Sarah's hand, "Maybe not. If Sarah agrees, we'll give you a year. I don't think it will make much difference to our plans. If all goes well we should be able to save a little extra to take with us."

They talked it over and after Sarah concurred, the three of us discussed it further. They were owed four weeks holiday and John thought Pub and Club would agree to them working two weeks and the remainder as holiday. I informed them that The Victory was not yet a done deal and they may consider it safer to hold on until I confirmed the purchase. Their present package was fifteen and a half thousand per annum and we agreed on eighteen thousand per annum plus twenty per cent of net profit, before tax. Generous, but they were the couple I wanted, and needed to make The Victory a success.

CHAPTER 35

After a chat with Joe Harrison the following Friday, it was decided my best way forward was to use a nominee company, as my shareholder, in a new limited company that would be formed to purchase The Victory. The nominee company would also act as director, and I would approach John and Sarah to be additional directors, although other than signing the odd document the task would not be to onerous. Control would remain with me through the nominee company and Joe had agreed to be company secretary.

It would take a week or two to set in motion and I advised Henry as soon as all was in place, contracts would be signed.

The two weeks turned in to four although there was a small problem with getting the bank to open accounts where the shareholder and main director were anonymous. Complications would only arise if the company wished to borrow but as this was not in my plans I could not envisage this difficulty happening.

The sale went through and as promised, I paid Henry an additional six thousand in cash. I had one other chore to carry out, or to get John to carry out on my behalf, and that was to speak with Jeanie and ask her how to get in touch with Henry's ex, Carol, so as to give her six thousand pounds, in order she got her fair share of the pub sale. Vic and Jeanie were well impressed with the new proprietor of The Victory.

Refurbishment included a small restaurant area and fitting of a new kitchen. There was ample space for expansion and there was a room to the back of the bar that was unused. A chef would be required and I told John that was his responsibility although if he needed advice to contact Max at Fat Dicks. Salary was to be no more than three hundred and fifty a week.

It was four months before work was completed, but the opening night, with the offer of a free drink and buffet, meant a good crowd attended. I remained in the background but was pleased to hear a number of people saying they would be returning. It felt odd to own a pub and yet the patrons thought that John and Sarah were the owners. I did however pull the first pint; after all, it was my pub. The recipient was a chap and his wife in their twenties. It is not often that I take a second glance at attractive young women, but this one with her shock of red hair, almost knocked me off my feet. At first, I thought she was a tall lass until I noticed the heels she was wearing. However, it was her eyes that drew me, unbelievably green. Having served the first customers in to the bar, I made myself scarce.

Business was brisk and in less than a month, The Victory, was once again the village pub. Turnover had risen from negligible to over eight thousand a month with a seventy thirty split between wet and food sales. Gross profit was just over sixty per cent for nine months. The figures were going the right way.

John and Sarah's twelve months were soon over and during their last two weeks, I made regular appearances in the pub, serving and getting to know the clientele a little better. I had not been a stranger at The Victory, but nobody had ever cottoned on that I was the owner. My chef was well established and the food he prepared was of a very high standard. I gave him the telephone number for Rebecca, the pepper pot lady, who provided the chutneys for The Old Bell and told him to use mine and Ben's name and see if he could get a deal the same as The Old Bell. I approached an agency for an experienced bar person and after a couple of not quite what I wanted experiences, employed a young Australian called Sue Roberts. Blonde with a bubbly personality, she was just what The Victory needed.

A few months passed and trade was still on the increase. The restaurant was always fully booked Friday and Saturday evenings and the Sunday Roast was always a sell out with many locals opting to eat in the bar when the restaurant tables were taken. Sue was a competent employee and even took care of choosing, and training where necessary, the part time staff.

Visits to my mother were now more regular and I noticed a slow decline in her demeanour. One positive was that she was well looked after by her carers. I often arranged my calls to coincide with the Leanne's visit as she kept me well informed of my mother's general health and well-being.

Life was going swimmingly until one day I was working the bar with Sue when Andy Strong walked in. He made straight to where I was serving.

"I heard you had your hands on this place. I don't know how you managed that without me finding out. Lets hope you can keep this place up together better than The Old Bell." He was sniggering as he spoke.

"Why Andy, you're a sight for sore eyes. Didn't think I'd ever see you again. Oh no, sorry it was your nephew that got put inside. I would say they got the wrong man but as he was doing your bidding then he deserved it. Pity he was too loyal to drop you in it. Now if you're not going to buy a drink then I'll have to ask you to leave." I gave him a sickly smile.

"You'll get yours Barker. One day when you're not looking. Could be nasty. And then I'll buy this place nice and cheap. Reckon this is a real money-spinner and it would suit me down to the ground."

I turned to the person stood next to him at the bar. "Did you hear that Bob. This bloke reckons I'm going to get mine one day when I'm not looking. Oh sorry Andy I should have introduced you, this is Bob Lloyd, he's the local bobby. Bob this is Andy Strong. He'd like to think he's a big noise in the underworld but he's more like a little prick in underpants."

Bob Lloyd faced Andy. "Must check his record when I get in tomorrow. Like to know what crim's are on my patch. Andy Strong you say, I'll remember that. Nice to meet you Andy and if you ever need to ask the way then ask a policeman. It should help keep you on the straight and narrow." These last words were directed to Andy's back as he left the pub.

"Have another pint Bob. Very handy you were standing at the bar when he came in."

"That's okay Chas I must make this my last one. I'm on duty later tonight."

"Fair enough but there's one behind the bar when you next call."

At three o'clock I got a call from Sue to say that somebody had thrown a brick through the lounge bar window. I told her I would deal with it in the morning. It was easy to guess who had thrown the brick, or arranged to have it thrown, but I did not see the point in talking to Andy. I would take a different approach.

It took me three days but I finally had an address for a small office block in Thatcham. There were four businesses resident there but the only one I was interested in was Edwards and Associates. The nameplate on the outside of the building indicated they were on the first floor. A sign at the top of the stairs pointed to the left. I entered in to a reception area through a half-glazed door where there was a young woman sat at a keyboard.

"I'd like to see Sally Edwards please."

"Do you have an appointment? Mrs Edwards doesn't see anybody without an appointment." She spoke without bothering to look up.

"No I do not have an appointment but I think she will want to see me. My name is Chas Barker."

"Without an appointment I don't think she will see you." She still had not looked up from whatever was so enthralling on her desk.

"Well you won't know if you don't ask her will you?"

She finally looked up and gave me a hard stare. "Who did you say were?"

"Tell her it's Chas Barker."

She picked up the phone and pressed a couple of buttons. "Mrs Edwards I have a Mr Barker here who says he wants to see you. I've him told you don't usually . . . ." Her voice tailed off and a moment later put the phone down. She looked at me. "Mrs Edwards said give her two minutes and she'll see you."

"Thank you." I replied and looked around for a chair to sit in.

I had barely sat down when a door opened and a woman in her late thirties with auburn hair appeared through it. As outside the court, the black eye make-up and pink lipstick was still a fixture. She had on a smart tailored skirt and jacket with a cream blouse. The make up did nothing to soften her features.

"Mr Barker what can I do for you? Come on through and take a seat. I thought our association finished when Troy was banged up. I don't hold a grudge against you for that, if it had been one of my businesses, I would have had the buggers legs."

I took a seat opposite her and smiled. "What, your own son?"

"Well may be not that, but you're a copper or at least you were. You are probably well aware of my record, although that may be a little strong, because I don't have a record. Why are you here?"

"To warn you to keep Andy under control, or he will be joining Troy. After a visit from him the other night I had a brick through the window in the early hours of the morning. Now I don't live on the premises but I do not expect my staff to be harassed by the likes of him.

I'm being polite at the moment and am asking nicely for it to stop. Like you, I know enough little tykes who for a tenner will start to toss bricks through your pubs and clubs and other premises. I don't need a turf war and neither do you. He's your brother, stop him before I do."

"You're right I don't need the aggravation and I will be having words with him. Send me the bill for the window and I will personally take the money off him in order to emphasize that what I tell him I mean."

"Thanks, I'll leave it your hands." We both got up and she walked me to door where she shook my hand and I left to return to The Victory.

Four days later a young courier driver delivered a letter to the pub containing thirty five pounds for the window repair and a bouquet of flowers for Sue with apologies for the nuisance caused.

CHAPTER 36

The months passed and there was no repetition of Andy's antics.

He did however visit one more time to inform me that one day The Victory would be his. I told him to dream on.

Following the departure of John and Sarah I was now the sole director through the nominee company and sole shareholder. The staff enjoyed a generous salary and I still distributed a portion of the profit between them.

Business at The Victory was improving month upon month. Sue was now managing the pub, and she had employed with my blessing, a barman. This relieved me of carrying out the heavier chores although I still dealt with the brewery reps and decided which beers we sold. Sue when available attended some meetings that usually took place over a light lunch.

A quite serious dilemma occurred which led to me having to hire a van and scurry around buying casks of ale and lager. For a reason, which I never discovered our usual Thursday delivery never happened, and after exchanging some unrepeatable words, with a manager at the brewery, I was promised a delivery for Friday afternoon. When this had not arrived by three thirty I again telephoned the brewery and spoke with the foreman, and getting no help from him, to the manager. He reiterated that the draymen had finished for the day and there would be no further deliveries. Despite my threats to speak to Harry Adams, a director who was known personally to me, they would not move on there stance.

They did however agree to stay at the brewery and let me have the some of my order, if I could find transport.

I was incensed and told them I would be down at the brewery by five o'clock and there had better be the best part of my usual delivery available with the rest to follow on Monday. A customer with a small haulage firm, provided me with a lorry and driver.

I managed to get hold of Frank, the brewery rep and told him he needed to call next Monday if he wished to retain my business. As it was, he appeared on the Saturday morning full of profuse apologies and promising to find out what had gone wrong.

As compensation, he told me there would be no charge for this week's delivery, and when I raged that there was no delivery because I had incurred the cost of hiring a man and a van and collecting my order, he sweetened the apology with two free kegs of lager every week for a year. Pushing him even harder I said for two years. The biggest surprise was he did not knock me back but agreed, provided my usual order did not decrease. I was not sure how I would manage to sell this extra beer, but if necessary, I would give it away.

As luck would have it a solution appeared within a few weeks.

About a mile down the road from The Victory is an Indian restaurant and I frequently popped in for a meal or picked up a take-away on the way home. I had got quite friendly with Jamshed, the owner and for what reason I do not know but we were discussing niggles we had with suppliers and breweries. I had mentioned my problem with the delivery a few months previously and it appeared that Jamshed who used an independent supplier also suffered the odd setback. He also found their prices extortionate.

Unexpectedly I received an offer to purchase The Victory from a business agent. The price mentioned was fair but I felt pretty sure the person behind this was Andy Strong, although the agent declined to divulge the name of his client. I turned down the offer and also mentioned I would not even entertain a sale even if the purchase price was increased.

Once again I had achieved my goal of buying and improving a pub and was now thinking of what I could do next.

My meeting with Joe Harrison confirmed what I already expected. Purchase and renovation of The Victory had eroded my capital. I had plenty of assets but was short on ready cash. Joe told me to give it a year or eighteen months, then consider selling The Victory and buying two pubs in need of a little TLC. The idea appealed to me.

CHAPTER 37

I set about making sure I got the best price possible for the pub. My belief was, that once I put The Victory on the market, then Andy Strong would be sniffing around,

I had been selling the free kegs of lager to Jamshed and had frittered away the cash but now I would use it to my advantage. Better still Jamshed often asked if I had extra and so I increased my own order by two kegs per week.

Fortuitously like all Aussies, Sue decided to move on and I took over the day to day running of the bar with the aid of the barman and additional bar staff. For my plan to succeed I would have to put in a lot of effort. The hours were long but I found enjoyment in my work.

"Bloody hell Chas you were up late last night weren't you. I came past the pub at well gone midnight last night and the lights were still on. Thought maybe you had a lock in and nearly stopped to join you, but Tina would have given me hell. She hates being on her own in the evenings." Steve was supping his third pint of the night.

"This ain't no nine to five job Steve. After I've thrown all you layabouts out I have to tidy round and do the till." Inwardly I had a little chuckle and thought, no, Tina doesn't like being on her own in the evenings, that's why on Mondays and Wednesdays I keep her company for a while. Mondays and Wednesdays were my keep fit nights but nobody had ever cottoned on as to where I was keeping fit.

"Thought you had staff to do that. Don't Ginny and Keith clear up after closing. No good having a dog and barking yourself." Steve laughed, then added, "Not that I think they're dogs. That Ginny is just what a barmaid should be. Is she the reason you're here so late in to the night?" He laughed again.

Steve was a likeable guy, a bit loud at times and often said the wrong thing at the wrong time. Did I feel guilty about having an affair with his wife? Not really, he spent every night in the pub and as Tina informed me, he would then go home and fall asleep, often downstairs in an armchair.

There was not any love between Tina and myself, just a mutual need and attraction, and what I thought was an absolute necessity, respect. She would never leave Steve and I had no intention of getting married.

Over the next few months the bar, and restaurant got busier, and I was now supplying Jamshed on a regular weekly order. Because he charged almost a pound a pint more than pub prices I was not concerned about competition.

On the odd occasion, there were enquiries about buying the pub including the infrequent call from Andy telling me he meant to have the pub eventually.

"It doesn't matter what you say, I intend to have The Victory as part of our portfolio of pubs and clubs. I'll even pay a little over the asking price, and then you can retire you must be at least fifty."

"Sorry Andy I'm not looking to retire and when you consider our history, then the last person I would wish to sell to, would be you." I knew why Andy wished to buy The Victory. Not only did he want what I had but he had started to push drugs and as this was the only pub within a few miles, he wanted it as an outlet.

I continued to put in the long hours and Joe informed me that the accounts were looking very good and month on month were increasing the saleability of the pub. Capital was also spent on extending the bar area and restaurant. I reckoned the value was shooting up.

Visits to my mother were now more sporadic but I had noticed a decline in her cognitive abilities, which was corroborated by the carers. I arranged for a visit by social services and this was followed by a report from an occupational therapist.

It confirmed my worst fears that her health was in serious decline. When I visited, although she would usually recognise me, she struggled to remember my name. Mood swings were also more apparent.

I had also received telephone calls from Fay, concerned that conversation between her and my mother was becoming difficult. I explained, and made her aware of the latest report I had received.

Fay wanted to fly back the next day, to do what I had no idea. She insisted that our mother needed her to care for her, but I managed to put her off, at least in the short term. To put her mind at rest I faxed a copy of the medical reports I had received and promised to call her if there was any change.

I had worked nine months continuous since Sue's departure and it was beginning to tell. As luck would have it a local girl who had done a substantial amount of bar work asked about some work and I offered her almost as many hours as she wanted. The bonus was her name was also Sue, so I did not have to get used to another name! Tired as I was, the relationships across the bar did not suffer, but there was many a morning when I really did not wish to get out of bed. Living at the pub was not as relaxing as being in my own house.

CHAPTER 38

Joe Harrison called me to lay out the facts regarding the two businesses. Both pubs were doing extremely well and he told me it was time to think again concerning my plans for the future. Did I want to sell The Victory and buy another one or two pubs, would I rather sell my share in The Old Bell to provide capital, or would I envisage borrowing against the two to produce the finance necessary for new purchases? My aim in life was now changing again and I was back to having to rethink my next move. Life was changing at a rapid speed and so were my thoughts on the future.

Fay called again and told me she had made up her mind and was returning home to care for my mother. I asked her what Ron her husband thought of this and was surprised to learn that they had parted eight years ago and divorced five years ago.

I was taken aback by this news. I know we spoke occasionally on the telephone but this had never been mentioned before. Did my mother know? He had left her well provided for, but she no longer had the desire to live in Spain, and at fifty-nine, was not looking for a second husband. She did not wish to discuss the details of their parting. Her property was in course of sale and she expected to be back in the UK in a few weeks. She would move in with mum and I agreed that would not cause any problems but we could discuss it, once she was back home.

This news alleviated one of my misgivings over my future plans and I now felt secure enough to proceed.

With no warning, I called at The Old Bell mid morning to meet with Ben and Jane and put a proposition to them. The Old Bell had been well run by the pair of them and all three of us were reaping the rewards of their labour. I found it difficult to gauge their reaction to my offer and told them there was plenty of time to think it over, if they considered a couple of months plenty of time.

Deciding now was the time to set wheels in motion I telephoned Browns. "Good morning. My name is Chas Barker; I'm thinking of putting my pub restaurant on the market and am wondering if you would be interested in acting as agents. No doubt you would wish to visit the premises and have a look at the accounts, before you make a decision."

"Good morning Mister Barker, I'm John Brown. I believe we've met before, probably a couple or so years ago. Give me a few details of the property and I'll tell you what I think."

He was right and we had met before. I had and still did think that he had conspired with Andy Strong to thwart my purchase of pubs in the vicinity.

"That's right. A short while ago I was looking at pubs in the Newbury area. Never lucky in getting one though, I was always outbid. Still if I'd got one of those, I'd have never got The Victory, and this has to be my best investment yet."

We discussed the premises and profitability of the business, and then got on to Browns commission. I managed to beat him down by a full one and a half per cent. We arranged that he would visit the pub the following day to assess the property and that I would provide a copy of the last audited accounts and up to date management accounts. I left his office with a smile on my face.

※

As soon as Chas had left the office John Brown picked up his telephone and dialled a number he knew by heart. "Andy, you remember that bloke trying to buy those pubs in Hermitage and Theale that you snapped up behind his back, or would have done if Sally hadn't stepped in, well, he's just been in to put The Victory up for sale. You did tell me to let you know if it ever came on the market. Not only is it on the market, but I am the sole agent."

"Has he indeed John. Thanks for keeping me in the picture, it won't be forgotten. How much is he asking for the place, I hope you're going to undervalue it?"

"No. I'll put a lowish valuation on it and tell him I already have an interested party if he wants a quick sale."

"Don't tell him it's me or he'll probably refuse to sell. I just want to see the look on his face when he realises I'm the buyer."

"Yeah, well that's alright but we haven't got it yet. Let's see what the valuation is. This deal is for you and me. Remember we agreed I could have a twenty-five per cent share in this venture. I hope you have the funds available to meet your share."

"Don't worry I have more than enough for this. Sal may think she's the brains in this family, but I've outsmarted her and siphoned enough out of the business to see me alright. You just screw Barker down and we'll come out of this laughing. I've watched this pub a few times, and popped in. It's an absolute gold mine, and will suit my purposes down to the ground. I'll come round to see you in a couple of days and we'll have a drink or two."

John spoke seriously, "Well if you've screwed that money out of Sally's business I hope you've covered your tracks well Andy, because if she find's out, your life won't be worth living. And I can't say that I would feel that secure, in fact you may not even live. You've seen what she's done to those that cross her in business. Shit, some of them have disappeared altogether. Probably got far away before she got her hands on them, but I wouldn't want to bet my life on it."

Andy laughed. "You worry too much. Sal is a pussycat really. She talks tough but she wouldn't harm family." Andy put the receiver down.

CHAPTER 39

Joe Harrison had already spoken to a colleague in the licensed trade and he conservatively valued The Victory at Eight hundred and fifty thousand pounds and The Old Bell at six hundred thousand. Chas could not believe the figures he was being quoted. This was far more than he had expected although Joe had told him a few months back that turnover was well up, and the gross figures were exceptional.

John Brown called as arranged at ten o'clock and I showed him around the public area, the bar and cellar side and the private accommodation upstairs. He told me he had already taken account of the garden and car park. I showed him the last three years audited accounts that showed year on year increased turnover and profitability despite ever increasing drawings.

"Wow!" he exclaimed, "You really have turned this place around and in such a short time, these figures are amazing. A short while ago I called by this place because I heard it may go on the market, and the place was abysmal."

"Well I can tell you it didn't happen overnight and a lot of blood, sweat and money has gone in to achieving where we are today. I'll expect a good price for this so give me an idea of a ball park figure."

Brown pursed his lips then looking around at the bar said, "The market is not as strong as it was last year and a business of this size has a limited market. However I do know someone interested in purchasing a going concern although he was not too keen on this area as he was looking for something closer to London, but he may be willing to think about it. I'll talk to him later and see what he says."

"Okay, that sounds interesting but what figure are we thinking about?"

"Around the six fifty mark. I may be able to push him a little higher."

"Um!" I replied, "That's not as high as I had hoped for but if you think that's the going price then I will have to consider his offer. Push him for seven fifty and see what he comes up with. At those figures, I'm inclined to put it on the market and see what offers come in."

"Okay Chas, I'll go back to the office see what I can work out on the valuation and then give him a call. I'll call you back as soon as I have an answer from him. Meanwhile I'll get something ready for the trade journals and web site. Are there any other questions, if not I'll be off and start to earn my crust."

"No John. Thanks for what you've done and I'll expect to get a call later. I should warn you that I do have two contacts of my own to telephone, who a few months ago asked me to call them if I ever wished to sell."

Brown looked concerned. "Well it's a little unusual and I would prefer to be involved in any sale. After all it is my livelihood."

I tried to appease him by saying, "Look if either of them decides to buy the place then I'll pay you half commission. I can't say fairer than that."

Once Brown was back in his office, he phoned Andy. "The bloke is not stupid Andy, he knows the rough value of his pub. I reckon we can get it for seven straight. I'll tell him I asked for seven twenty five and that was your offer. I reckon the place is worth at least eight seven five maybe even nine two five, plus of course stock. The turnover for that place is astonishing and his gross at nearly sixty-four per cent is fantastic. The place is a gold mine. The only drawback is there may be another punter, but we'll wait and see."

"Okay John, I'll leave it up to you but I don't want to lose this place. I'll show Sally that I am just as fucking clever as her."

"Alright, I'll phone him in the morning with our offer and see what his response is. Keep your cheque book handy, you're going to need it."

After he'd put the receiver down he waited an hour and then called Chas to say he been in touch with his client, Freddie Smith, and he said he would think it over and let him know in the morning. Smith would like an early viewing if he decided in favour.

His next call was to an old school chum Jolyon Hardcastle, who liked to think of himself as a great actor, although he was an estate agent who liked to take part in amateur dramatics. He also had two ex wives and was always short of money.

The following morning Brown telephoned to say his client, Freddie Smith, had made an offer of seven hundred thousand. He would like to view the premises within the next few days if possible.

Chas made some uming and ahing over the telephone then replied, "Not as much as I was hoping for but if there are no further enquiries over the next four or five weeks then I may well accept."

"I think Mister Smith was expecting a quick response to his offer Mister Barker. I know he is looking at pubs closer to his base in West London."

"That was a quick response," Chas came back with, "Maybe not the one he wants but I'm not taking the first offer until I've seen what the market offers. I'm also waiting to hear back from my two contacts, one of which is very keen. He's holidaying in the Maldives at the moment but will be back next week and will call me then."

"Okay I'll go back to him and let him know your decision. I understand your position but in the meantime, I'll try to keep him sweet. What about the viewing, later this week or early next? Maybe once he's seen the property, he will wish to increase his offer."

"Don't mind. I shall be here all the time so if you could give me a days notice, that will be ample. And by the way, call me Chas."

Brown rang off and called Andy to let him know the response to the offer. "He didn't bite at seven, so we may have to increase our offer. I'm not going to do anything at the moment; I'll let him return to me."

CHAPTER 40

Brown and Smith arrived just after three thirty on the Thursday afternoon and introductions were made. After viewing the premises from outside Smith cast an eye over the accommodation which although clean and tidy was a little dated.

Freddie Smith spoke first. "The exterior is ship shape but the upstairs is in need of renovation, and that could cost a fair penny. Still that's not what matters, what really interests me is your barrelage. John gave me a breakdown of your last audited accounts and management figures and I'll admit they look pretty impressive. What I'm looking for is a place that allows for expansion, do you see an opportunity for that?"

"You can see from the space available at the side of the car park, that the restaurant could be added to and I have done little with the garden which could prove to be a family environment, especially in the summer, with barbeques etcetera. If I was to stay then that is probably what I would do. However, my mother's health has deteriorated and she needs my attention now."

"Sorry, I didn't realise. I thought you were selling to move on and redevelop another pub." Smith sounded genuine. "Is your mother okay?"

"Just old age coupled with dementia. Other than that, she's quite fit. Problem is she can no longer carry out the simplest of duties and needs somebody with her twenty-four hours a day. She could go in to a home but if possible, I'd like to avoid that. Anyway to get back to The Victory, what do you think?"

"I'll admit it's a nice set up, and I do like the place, but of course at the right price." Smith cast his eye around the bar again, where Sue was preparing for the evening trade. "Do you mind if I sit here for a while and watch."

John Brown had forewarned me that Smith used to like to watch the workings of the pub and I did not mind, in fact, I relished the idea. "No, I'm quite happy for you to enjoy the place. Would you like another cup of tea or would you prefer something stronger?" He settled for a gin and tonic.

An hour or so passed and there was a steady stream of early evening drinkers, popping in for a quick pint before going home for tea, the missus and the kids. This was followed by the influx of the more serious drinkers, interspersed with others, wishing to use the restaurant. I moved to the other side of the bar to give Sue a hand.

John Brown seemed a little bored by it all but Smith seemed impressed. He beckoned me to the end of the bar. "Well having seen this operation, I would like to increase my offer to seven hundred and fifty thousand, but I would like a response by Monday. That will give you tomorrow and the weekend to think it over."

I agreed that he could have my answer by Monday.

Late on Friday afternoon I received a call from John Brown. "Good afternoon Chas. I have good news for you. A Mister Jones has put in an offer of seven hundred and seventy five thousand pounds. This is a very good offer and I have informed Freddie Smith that if he is still interested then he will need to increase his offer. I am waiting to see what his response will be." There was not a lot of enthusiasm in his voice for this good news.

※

"Eight hundred fucking thousand! You said maybe seven twenty five, now you're telling me it's eight hundred thou. Do you know what you're doing John, 'cos I'm beginning to fucking doubt it. I want that place and I want to see the contracts signed and then I can walk in there just to see the look on Barker's face when he realises I've just bought his precious pub."

"Andy, I never expected to receive another offer so soon on top of the one from Freddie Smith. Jolyon played the part well and I thought that by Monday, it would be in the bag. I'll leave it till Monday afternoon then tell him Smith will increase his offer to eight hundred. It will still be cheap even at that price. His beer taps must be continually running, Barrelage is fantastic. Even on a Thursday early evening the place was busy with punters. We won't lose money on this even if we pay a million."

"A million! You've got to be fucking joking. That'll take just about every penny I can lay my hands on, and more. Keep him below nine hundred, I can manage that, just about."

"Is that the limit I have to work to Andy? I don't want to put in an offer you can't meet."

"All I want is for you to get me that pub as cheaply as possible. If another arsehole phones with an offer, don't tell Barker."

※

"Thanks Ben. I think your offer has made Strong have to think again. I'm pretty sure that Smith is a front for him. When we were sat here discussing the business I had this realization that he knew no more about the pub trade than most of my customers. Somebody had told him what questions to ask and to begin with, it sounded plausible, but when we were sat having a drink he was asking how many pints I sold and how many bottles of wines and spirits. He already had the barrelage for the various items but seemed to forget his lines once he'd had a drink and started to relax. Luckily, at this stage Brown was involved in conversation with Steve Hunt and a couple of his mates who were here making the pub look busy. Thank your locals for popping in to swell numbers. As promised they will all receive their hard earned cash back, plus some."

"They'd have done it for nothing Chas, the same as I and Jane are willing to do. You don't have to give me and Jane anything. You did us a big favour letting us have control of this place. I know we all benefit but we could never have got our foot on the ladder without your help."

"You both worked hard for what you have, and it hasn't done me any harm either. Anyway enough of that, I just wanted to say thank you very much. I'll be in touch later, meanwhile buy all those good enough to call in Thursday night a drink on me. I'll settle up with you later. And don't forget I am still waiting for a response to my last offer."

We said our goodbyes and I returned to bottling up for the evening, before Sue arrived.

The weekend went well and Andy showed his face during the Sunday lunchtime opening. He did not speak to me but bought himself a pint and sat quietly in one corner just looking around. I did not see him go. His manner as good as confirmed to me that he was my Freddie Smith.

CHAPTER 41

On Monday morning, I telephoned John Brown. I was going to leave it until the afternoon but Andy's visit the day before told me that early would be better.

"Hi John, had a visit from one of the friends I told you was interested in The Victory and he told me he was willing to pay nine hundred thousand. I can't believe that a few days ago we were looking at seven hundred thousand. I think I should accept and get the solicitors involved. I shouldn't think anybody will top that figure. It's unbelievable. His name is Vic Yorke and I've passed on your number for him to contact you."

"Don't be to hasty Chas. Are you sure he has the money available for a purchase of this size, and don't forget there's the stock to be added to that figure."

Oh, I know he's got the wherewithal for that amount. His old man is loaded and is like a silent partner in his dealings. No, I'm not concerned that he wouldn't be able to pay. We've known each other too long for him to try and dupe me."

"Well that's good to know but just to be fair to the other two prospective purchasers; I think we should give them a final bite at the cherry so to speak. If you agree I'll phone them as soon as we finish speaking."

※

"What I've done Andy is call this Jones character and tell him that I need to know if he wishes to increase his offer. I've tried to pin him down to a three day deadline. Once I have his figure we can submit one a little higher. Hopefully this new party won't want to go any higher."

"That's alright but this is becoming a nightmare John. I thought that we'd make a decent offer and Barker would jump at it. Every time you phone me, it costs another hundred thousand. With your funds maxed out at three fifty, it leaves me to find the extra, and I'm scraping the barrel. I can't take any more out of Sal's business or she'll notice. You need to close this sale off and bloody quickly."

"You have to realise that The Victory is a very good business with room for expansion if required. Did you know he has looked at purchasing the land and bungalow next door. He was thinking of adding rooms and turning the place in to a hotel! I originally placed it on the market with a guide price of offers in excess of seven hundred thousand. So far, there has been numerous enquiries but when informed of the latest offer, then interest dwindled. Now there are just three parties looking to purchase, and we are in a good position."

"We're not in any position until the contracts are signed. You need to earn your crust John or we will end up with bugger all." Andy put his receiver down ending the call.

※

I made a call to Fay to find out what progress had been regarding her repatriation. Sale of property and the tax situation was different to the UK, which was causing her some concern. However a friend who had already returned to the UK had given her the name of a retired Englishman who was helping her sort out any problems as they arose.

"How long before you think everything will be settled and you can return home? Mum doesn't fully comprehend a lot of what she's told but she does say she will be glad to have you home with her."

Fay laughed. "You mean she wants somebody to wait on her and I will do. Be truthful Chas, what is she really like? Is she clean? You know, toileting and washing."

"You've no need to worry; you'll have all the help you need. Do you remember Leanne from your last visit? She takes care of mum as if she was her own granny. Mum responds to her probably more than she will to you. The other carers who cover her time off are good but Leanne just has that something extra. Watch out for the odd bit of cussing and four lettered words that creep in when she gets a little upset. Other than that, she's your mother, you'll cope. If she starts sounding off at you, ignore it and don't try to argue with her, it only acts to spur her on. Take each day one at a time and enjoy your time with her, you can't do more."

"You really know how to inspire me Chas. If I listen to you any longer I shall stop the sale of my property and stay here."

"No you won't. Plus I've offered you an unbeatable deal on my house. It will enable you to have a property here in the UK, and as your living with mum, you can let it and give yourself a good income."

"I know, although for the life of me I can't fathom out why you want me to buy your house. Where are you going to live? What's the big secret, are you going bankrupt?"

I took some time explaining to Fay that I was selling my pub and my plans for the future. When she heard the amount, she could not believe my luck, or as I told her, my reward for my hard work. I told her I could not have assets in the UK as I was hoping to avoid paying tax on my ill-gotten gains.

Late that afternoon John Brown telephoned. "I've spoken to Vic Yorke, Ben Jones and Freddie Smith. Unfortunately although Ben Jones increased his offer to nine two five, he was topped by Freddie Smith at nine forty. Both your friends, Vic and Ben Jones decided they had gone far enough. The ball is now in your court to make a decision as to whether to accept Smith's offer. He said to let you know he will not go any higher. My advice is to accept. This price is far higher than I or I think even you expected."

"Thank you John, I believe that to be very good advice so you can tell Freddie he has a pub. I'll let my solicitor and accountant know and to ask them to contact you for any further details they may want. Again thank you very much, I owe you a drink. I'll be in contact again shortly." I rang off and burst out laughing.

Picking the receiver back up I rang Joe to tell him my news. He sounded flabbergasted. "I don't believe that price. It's a nice pub but I would have guessed seven fifty."

I smiled to myself and thought, "Even that sounds a little high, but then the Andy Strong relevance had not been considered by anybody but me." Speaking out loud, "Fairy tale figures Joe but then why should I complain. Once contracts are exchanged and before completion, I will need to see you Joe as I will require some help and advice."

We chatted a little more then agreed to speak again in a day or so.

Legal matters, searches, draft contracts and the toing and froing of solicitor's letters took four weeks. It was another week before acceptable contracts were exchanged, allowing a deduction of ten thousand pounds to allow for renovation of the upstairs accommodation. Ten thousand pounds was nothing to me and I was sure it gave Andy a feeling of accomplishment. Finally contracts were signed by both parties with completion in four weeks.

The evening of the exchange of contracts, Andy showed his face in the pub. Before he could say anything I offered him my hand. "Let me buy you a drink Andy, today I sold The Victory. Sorry but a Freddie Smith bought it, so you'll have to wait a bit longer to own it."

He took my hand. "Oh, don't you worry I'll get my hands on this place one day, maybe even sooner than you think, and thanks I'll have a lager top."

I got him his lager top, and then moved down the bar to serve another customer. He stayed for another pint, then placing his empty glass on the bar, rose from his stool, and went to the door, turned and waved, with a smirk on his face. Inside I was laughing and thinking I know something you do not Mister Strong.

CHAPTER 42

The hand over was to take place on a Monday morning with the pub remaining closed until the evening, by which time the new owners managers would be installed.

There was one surprise I did not expect.

"Hi Chas or is it Charlie." The person speaking the words was none other than Pat from The Black Horse at Caversham.

Quickly gathering my wits about me, I replied, "Well! Well! Pat you old rogue, do the magistrates still see fit to give you licence? I'm surprised to see you. Does Freddie Smith know of your past? Still the past is the past, and I'll wish you best of luck for the future, as I would have for any new manager coming in."

The one thing I did expect was Andy to show his face, and I was not disappointed. He breezed in as if he owned the place, which I suppose he now did.

Not wishing to give the game away, I moved toward him. "Hi Andy come to welcome your old pal in to his pub?"

"Not quite, meet the new owner of The Victory." Andy put out his hand to shake mine and trying to look mystified, I hesitated a little in returning his gesture.

"You!" I exclaimed. "I thought Freddie Smith was the owner. How come you think you're the owner?"

With a grin a mile wide he answered, "Subterfuge Chas. Nothing but skulduggery and trickery. Freddie Smith is a bit part actor who played his part well. Hope there are no hard feelings, I told you I would own this pub one day, and now I do."

Keeping a straight face, to make sure the amusement I was enjoying did not show, I responded, "No! No hard feelings you won the battle fair and square, even if you did cheat a little." Then thinking to myself, "But not as much as me."

The handover was completed successfully and I left before the evening session was over. Sue was being kept on and after a hug and a few tears on her part, I departed for the final time. Just one or two loose ends to tie up and I would be on my way.

The monies from the sale of The Victory and the funds from Ben and Jane for purchase of The Old Bell had also come through. My house in Wokingham was being transferred in to Fay's name.

Ben and Jane had purchased the remaining sixty per cent of the issued shares of The Old Bell at a discounted price based on the earlier valuation of four hundred thousand although a truer value was nearer six hundred thousand.

I lay back in the spa pool at the Travelodge in a small town called Garberville on Route 101 in Northern California. At one time, Garberville was the cannabis centre of the universe and even today, the aroma of marijuana could be caught on the nostrils just by walking down the street. Not as strong as the pungent smell hits you in New Orleans, but it was still there. So, I think were most of the hippies that occupied Garberville in the nineteen sixties although they looked aged now.

I had only stopped for one night as I travelled north from San Francisco to explore the Redwoods, but had enjoyed the first night so much I had now been here for three days. I intended to spend some time exploring America before deciding if I anticipated buying a business and trying my hand in the U S of A.

My monies had been distributed in various banks in offshore accounts and I was unable to return to the UK unless I wished to risk a demand from Her Majesty's Tax Collectors. I could still visit for up to ninety days a year, with care.

Joe who set up the mechanics of my leaving telephoned regularly and kept me abreast of the situation at home. Andy Strong had already accused him of submitting false accounts but all the figures tied up and could be proven.

Why did pub sales look so good for The Victory? That was simple. Every keg sold to my friend Jamshed at the Indian restaurant was passed through the till as individual pints. Since deciding on the course of action I was to undertake, Jamshed's weekly order had risen to five kegs. Originally I used to deliver the casks to Jamshed, but as his order grew, he arranged for his two sons to collect and return the empties. I had worked in to the small hours many nights running those pints through the till!

It was agreed that after I had sold The Victory he would buy direct from the brewery. Frank my brewery rep was more than happy to find a new customer, especially as Jamshed was opening a further restaurant, which would need servicing as well.

By now Andy must be wondering where the sales had disappeared too, and just how much he had overpaid for the pub he had to have at any cost.

EPILOGUE

Two years had passed since Chas had relocated to California. A police raid on premises in Mortimer had discovered large amounts of hard drugs and the owner and the manager were both in custody pending trial.

Sally visited Andy whilst he was being held, just the once.

She let Andy know she had planted the drugs and tipped off the police and he could now experience life inside just like her son Troy. Initially, she told him, she had accepted that Troy's misfortune was partly of his own making, but later discoveries regarding Andy and over a million pounds of company funds missing, had decided her mind on taking a little retribution.

She would be buying The Victory at a much reduced price as it would help to set off the discrepancies she found in the accounts. She told Andy she was looking forward to the trial, especially the sentencing.

ACKNOWLEDGEMENTS

These are not really acknowledgements but thanks and recognition to various people in my life, who have provided inspiration and friendship during the period I was writing this novel. And for being kind enough to read my scribbling, Julie Wilcock, for the final perusal of my epistle, looking for my mistakes. I know it is time consuming and mind numbing. Because of all that is happening in your life, which makes your time precious, thank you. As you rightly point out, I have taken liberties, especially with the streets and names used.

Sarah Barker who after a long struggle against cancer, is finally at peace. You were a lovely lady and wonderful friend.

Ian Shone, who has suffered a brain tumour, but with the strength of his family and friends is well on the way to recovery.

Rebecca Raphael, who in a short space of time became a very good friend, and introduced me to some excellent Caribbean cuisine.

Sandra Tomlin. Never having met, you trusted me with knowledge of forthcoming surgery, and the responsibility of keeping a watchful eye on your daughter, separated from you by thousands of miles. For me that was so humbling. I look forward to meeting you when you visit the UK next year.

Errol Callender-Laffin. Your one failing is being a Gooner, but you are a lovely guy, so for that you are forgiven. Actually Leanne says you have more than one failing.

Leanne Tomlin. A more sensitive, caring person you would struggle to find. Mature beyond your young age, you are enchanting and charm all that you meet. Many of the new friends I have made in the past year or so are down to you. Thank you for your friendship. You have given me both joy and sadness in varying degrees. PS I still cannot figure out why you would want an old fart, forty years your senior, as a friend.

To my family and many other friends of old, I can add no more than the final words at the end of this passage.

To all of you. THANK YOU.

Lightning Source UK Ltd.
Milton Keynes UK
UKOW04f0204191213

223331UK00002B/25/P

9 781491 883501